To Richlie Fikes

Because you always asked me what was going to happen next...

UnEnchanted

An Unfortunate Fairy Tale

Chanda Hahn

ISBN-13: 978-1475070309
ISBN-10: 1475070306
UNENCHANTED
Copyright © 2012 by Chanda Hahn
Revised Edition 4-26-13
Photo by Jorge Wiegand
Cover Model Paulina Godoy
Cover design by Steve Hahn

www.chandahahn.com

UnEnchanted

CHAPTER 1

Today I saved Brody Carmichael's life!

Mina penned the jubilant words into her blue spiral notebook with her favorite ballpoint pen. She faithfully used the same pen when writing all of her entries in the hope that it would change her luck and she could write something good in her notebook—like today. Mina stared at the words written before her in her sloppy script and felt a pang of guilt. She started to close the notebook but paused in thought. It didn't feel right. It didn't seem…truthful. With a heavy hand and a heavy heart, she added in parentheses next to her previous entry:

(Today was also the day I almost KILLED Brody Carmichael).

Feeling slightly better about telling the truth, she closed her notebook, titled "Unaccomplishments and Epic Disasters," and tucked it in her dresser drawer with a sigh.

Nothing in the world ever went right for fifteen-year-old Mina. She was always late for class, her homework usually looked as if it had spent the evening being a chew toy for a pit bull when she didn't even own a dog, her long-time crush didn't know she existed, and she frequently spilled chocolate milk on herself whenever she became nervous. Mina was certain it was because she was the magnet for all the bad, terrible, and so-so luck that existed in the world, and therefore kept a notebook hidden in her unorganized sock drawer to prove it.

All of these events turned her into a cynic, especially since yesterday morning had started out like any other event-filled, disastrous day.

***

She dreamed she was flying. She was much more graceful in the air than on the ground, where her feet always seemed to be tripping her up. But her peaceful dream was interrupted by the loud banging and crashing of thunder. She was no longer flying…but falling.

"Ouch! What the…?" Mina cried out as she landed painfully on the mismatched oak wood floor of her bedroom. She had fallen out of bed. Struggling to untangle herself from her sheets and comforter, Mina saw a pair of feet poking out of blue *Toy Story* pajamas next to her head.

"Charlie, what are you doing?" she mumbled, still wrestling with her sheets.

Charlie, a young and solemn boy of eight, pointed toward her clock, which was blinking 12:00 p.m. In his hands he held a pot and wooden spoon. The power must have gone out again, which was a regular occurrence for their city block.

"What time is it?" she asked, feeling dread build, knowing that today she was going to be late…again.

Charlie held up one hand, pinching his ring finger and thumb together to sign the number seven.

"Charlie, how could you have let me sleep in so long? I'm going to be late!"

Charlie answered by shrugging his shoulders and banging on the pot with his wooden spoon. She knew that it wasn't Charlie's fault; she was a very deep sleeper. Her mother, Sara, said that she was harder to wake up than Sleeping Beauty. In Mina's case, though, there was no Prince Charming to rescue her from her snoring, and with her horrible luck, there never would be.

Jumping up, Mina grabbed what she hoped was a clean pair of jeans from the pile of clothes that littered her floor and slid into them. Silently she thanked her mother for never giving in to her request for skinny jeans; otherwise, her dressing time would have doubled. Next, she shoved her feet into her favorite Converse All Stars, bending the backs in the process.

Picking up a blue zippered hoodie, she gave it a cursory sniff before deeming it clean enough to wear. She ran her fingers through her long brown hair, attempting to tame the stray locks, which were the same boring color as her eyes. She tried to force a winning smile onto her face, but it slid into an awkward grimace.

Giving a quick kiss on her brother's head, she ran into the small and dated kitchen, and grabbed her backpack from the breakfast table. Turning, Mina heard a rip as the backpack clung stubbornly to the back of the chair. The chair won, and the shoulder strap ripped off the back of the bag, causing all of her books to crash to the floor in a heap.

Sighing, she threw each book back into the bag and did her best to hold it shut while she scoured the kitchen drawers for safety pins.

Sara Grime walked into the kitchen with a quizzical look on her face. She was dressed in her work clothes, tan pants and a blue polo with a stitched outline of a feather duster and smiling mop. Sara worked for Happy Maids, cleaning homes so she could afford the tuition to send Charlie to a private school. Their mother worked long hours without ever complaining, which was why Mina never allowed her to enter Mina's pigsty of a room.

"Mom, did you sign my permission form?"

"What permission form?" Sara asked distractedly, sliding a raspberry Pop Tart into the toaster.

"For today's field trip. To Babushka's Bakery, remember? I gave it to you last week."

"Oh, honey." Sara wrung her hands. "Don't you think it would be better if you didn't go on the field trip? You know how clumsy you are. What if something should happen to you?"

"Mom, I have a paper to write on today's trip, and it's worth a quarter of my grade." Mina had finally found a few safety pins in a junk drawer and was fumbling with them to reattach the strap to her backpack. She knew they didn't have enough money to buy another one. She would have to make do with a quick mend.

"Well, maybe you could do some extra credit instead?" Sara asked.

"Mom, I'll be fine. I'll stick to Nan like glue, and you won't have to worry about me. It's just a boring bakery tour. What could possibly go wrong, other than I die of boredom?" Mina saw the look on her mom's face and knew that she had won the argument...barely.

Going to a stack of mail by the fridge, Sara sifted through it until she found the folded yellow permission form. Signing it, she handed it to Mina with one last warning. "Just promise me you'll be careful."

"I will," Mina promised, knowing it was a half-truth. She would be careful, but bad luck had a habit of following her everywhere.

Charlie shuffled into the kitchen still wearing his pajamas, plus a striking pair of bright yellow galoshes. Sitting on a slightly dented chair, he pulled one of the boxes of cereal toward him and began his morning routine of combining random cereals into one bowl. Today he chose Franken Berry, Cheerios, and Grape-Nuts, a far cry from his normal combination of at least five cereals. Watching him mix cereal every morning made her stomach drop in disgust, which was why she preferred Pop Tarts.

The toaster released her Pop Tart and Mina grabbed it in midair, wishing she hadn't as she began tossing it back and forth in her hands until it cooled. Once it had cooled enough, it went into her mouth while she slipped on her temporarily fixed backpack and darted out the door to grab her bike from the landing.

The Grime family lived in a small rented apartment above The Golden Palace, a Chinese restaurant run by Mr. and Mrs. Wong. Mina loved living above the restaurant, unless she forgot to close her window the night before; then all of her clothes would smell like peanut oil. To make up for it, Mrs. Wong gave Mina all the pot stickers she could eat.

Mina carried the bike down the stairs to the sidewalk, nicking the paint from the wall on the way down. She had a love-hate relationship with the bike. Last year, on the eve of her fifteenth birthday, she thought she was being led outside blindfolded to be presented with a car. Instead she got a red 1950 Schwinn. The bike was old, scuffed, and needed new brakes, oil, and tires, but she didn't care.

Once she got over the disappointment, and realized how unrealistic a car would be on her family's budget, she began to love it. The bike allowed her some freedom. Besides, if Mina's riding ability was any indication of her driving ability, then the world would have been in for a lot of dented mailboxes.

Swinging her bike onto the sidewalk, Mina waved to Mrs. Wong and barely missed colliding into an old lady walking her gaggle of toy poodles. "Sorry!" she yelled, losing a chunk of the Pop Tart she was still holding in her mouth. She watched in disgust as the poodles, who only minutes ago looked cute and cuddly, morphed into snapping, sugar-crazed dogs. The lady stared in shock as she tried to get control of her wild, pampered babies. Mina shrugged apologetically in response.

Ten minutes later, after cutting through two back streets and riding across three neighbors' backyards, Mina arrived at a schoolyard that was devoid of human life, giving her the undeniable impression that she was tardy. She left her bike by the bike rack, but without a proper kickstand it sagged pathetically to one side against the nicer, newer bikes.

Running toward the bus barn, she was relieved to see the field trip bus was still there—until it pulled away from the curb.

"No!" Mina yelled, running after the bus, trying desperately to catch the notice of the driver.

A window slid down, and a familiar blonde head popped out with something silver in her hand. "Mina, you really need to get a watch," the girl shouted.

"Nan! Tell him to stop!" Mina cried, feeling a stitch begin in her side.

"And a cell phone! You really need to be brought out of the dark ages. I could have called you." The girl just kept talking, impervious to Mina's desperation and waning stamina.

"NAN! Snap out of it! Stop the bus!" she screamed, huffing and puffing.

"Oh, right!" The blonde head popped back inside. A moment later the bus slowly decelerated and pulled to the curb.

Out of breath, and slightly limping from the side stitch, Mina finally boarded the first steps of the bus. The bus driver gave her an indignant look; this would probably delay their arrival, and he was a stickler for being on time. She ignored him and stepped to the front row where her teacher was sitting to hand him her permission form.

"You really should have been on time," Mr. West commented. His balding head glistened from the heat of the already too-warm bus.

"I'm sorry," Mina answered quietly. "We had a power outage."

Mr. West looked over her permission form and then nodded for her to take a seat. Walking toward the back of the bus was like being in a bad slow-motion dream. She had no choice but to be the recipient of twenty-some odd stares.

Ducking her head and sliding into the seat next to Nan, Mina poked her in the side in revenge. "That's for making me run for so long."

Nan grinned, showing perfect white teeth. Today she was wore an "I <3 Jacob Black" shirt, skinny jeans, and black flats. Nan was the exact opposite of Mina in every way, which was why they probably got along so well. She got a kick out of Mina's lack of knowledge in all things social and popular.

"Well, maybe if you got a cell phone, you could have texted me you were running late," Nan quipped, pulling out her latest iPhone, fingers flying over the touchpad.

"What are you doing? Are you chirping?"

Nan rolled her eyes and laughed. "Really, Mina, it's called tweeting."

"Okay. Are you tweeting?"

"Of course." Nan smirked.

Mina's stomach sank. "About what?" She had a feeling she already knew the answer. She'd seen something in Nan's hand when she had previously opened the window and leaned out.

"Oh, nothing much. I'm just tweeting the picture of you running like a madman after the bus to all of my followers."

"Followers" made it sound like some sort of cult.

"Nan, how many followers do you have?" She hoped the number hadn't gone up.

"Well, after yesterday's rant about the garbage they pass off as lunch, I'm up to about three hundred." She clicked "Update," and immediately chiming could be heard from multiple phones on the bus. Snickers and heads turned Mina's way, and she heard whispers of "*loser*" and "*nerd.*"

"Nan! How could you?" Mina said, scrambling over Nan so she could be by the windows and out of direct line of sight to most of the riders. She pulled her backpack up over her head and hid behind the bag.

"Mina, you need to learn to laugh at yourself. I'm trying to get you noticed. Hardly anybody knows who you are."

"I can't imagine anyone wanting to be the center of *that* kind of attention. I certainly wouldn't."

Nan raised one eyebrow in disbelief. "Nonsense. Everyone wants to get at least some attention. Well, except for you. Really, Mina, it doesn't even matter whether it's good or bad, true or untrue—everyone wants to be popular, to be part of some gossip."

Nan was the friendliest and most outgoing girl in the school. Everyone seemed to like Nan, not because she was popular or smart, but because she was fun and real.

"Not me." Mina shrugged nonchalantly.

"So I guess in that case you wouldn't care about the current eligibility status of a certain boy?" Nan knew that her best friend had had a secret crush on Brody Carmichael ever since her family moved here.

"Brody and Savannah broke up?" Mina sat up straight in disbelief, knocking her backpack to the floor.

"Ah-ha! See, you are interested."

"No, I'm not," she said.

"Yes, you are," Nan taunted. She was right; Mina did want to know.

"Okay, fine… Did they?" Mina felt a flower of hope start to bloom and then shrivel up dead at Nan's next statement.

"No, but see! Wouldn't you want to know if they did?"

"I hate you, Nan Taylor!" Mina shot out. "You're a dream-killer, you know that right? Dream KILLER."

"Gee, Grimy, keep it down," a male voice shot out from behind their seat.

Her face flushed red. Mina hated her last name, an easy target for name-calling: Grime too easily translated to Slime, Brine, Grimy. She couldn't wait until she got married and could legally change her name…if she could ever overcome her awkwardness and talk to a boy.

Sitting back, she let Nan talk on about the latest episode of *Glee* and even sang a few bars from the new hit single she downloaded on her iPhone. Mina didn't even own an iPod; the closest thing she had was an old CD player. That was something else about Nan—she was addicted to *Glee* and every popular reality show on TV. Mina didn't understand her best friend's infatuation. Mina's own life was already a reality show; why would she want to watch someone else's?

The bus reached Babushka's Bakery, and all of the wary and bored teenagers filed off and waited in groups. This was Mina's chance to scan the crowd and find the tall blond-haired Brody Carmichael. Sure enough, he was standing next to

Savannah White, who looked every bit a princess with her long white-blonde hair, porcelain skin, and big blue eyes. Brody seemed distracted as Savannah latched possessively onto his arm, marking her territory as only a female high school student could.

Brody was the fantasy of every girl's dream. He was a perfectly blended cocktail of aristocrat and jock. The Carmichaels prided themselves on family lineage and could follow their ancestors back to when they first came over on the *Mayflower*. They raised racehorses, owned a clothing company, and were by far the richest family in the state. Yet Brody never let it get to his head. He never raised his voice, never bullied anyone, and seemed completely oblivious to his social status and effect on girls.

Her daydreaming was interrupted as a plump man hurried out of the gray brick factory.

"Welcome, children, we are so glad to have you here at Babushka's world-famous bakery. You can call me B.J.," the man said, smiling and wiping what looked like leftover powdered doughnut from his face. "Let me introduce your tour guide, Claire. She will take you around the factory and answer any questions you have."

The tour guide, a striking blonde woman named Claire, walked out of the factory in a form-fitting white lab jacket, yellow helmet, and goggles, which did virtually nothing to impede her leggy, model-like beauty. There were some obvious whistles and jabs among the boys, and even Brody stood a few inches taller within her presence. She smiled warmly at them, red lips framing perfect white teeth, and motioned the class to follow her into the factory. Her hips sashayed, and her red heels clicked on the cement sidewalk to a rhythm that only she could hear.

The boys followed like puppies, mere inches behind the tour guide, while the popular girls, including Savannah, hung back, shooting hateful glares toward Claire. A challenge had clearly been drawn without one spoken word, and the girls flipped their hair, powdered their noses, and glossed their lips in preparation to retaliate. Mina felt a moment of pity for the poor tour guide; she had personally seen what it was like to be on the receiving end of jealous girls from Kennedy High.

Mina looked at Nan to see if she noticed, but Nan was preoccupied with her texting. Taking a deep breath, Mina grabbed Nan's sleeve and led her after the group of students into the factory with Nan texting the whole way.

Claire took them through a fluorescent-lit hallway lined with photo murals of Babushka's Bakery's history. She paused every few feet to explain the history, as Mina grabbed a chewed-up pencil and notebook out of her broken backpack and struggled to catch up. "This is our founder, Larry Brimwell. In 1911, he started the bakery out of his two-bedroom home, and later moved it into a rented building in the international district in 1913." A grainy black-and-white photo could be seen of a man with a white apron and hat, rolling small balls of chocolate on a small kitchen table. Out of focus and barely visible underneath the table was a small brown-haired boy playing with a wooden car.

The next wall mural depicted a smiling Mr. Brimwell outside a small vacant building with a "For Rent" sign in the dirty, paned window. A severe, unsmiling blonde woman stood next to Mr. Brimwell, one hand holding a small clutch purse. This was obviously his wife, holding the hand of their little boy. Mina stopped to stare at the picture of what was supposed to be a happy family, but the picture seemed odd, almost forced. Mina wondered what was really going on in Mrs. Brimwell's mind.

"It was Mrs. Brimwell who saw the potential of turning the bakery into a full-scale factory and invested all of her inheritance in the company against her father's wishes. Soon after they purchased this current factory, Larry died of scarlet fever. His wife and son were left to take on the family business alone." Claire stopped speaking, her voice quavering for only a split second, before she cleared her throat and dazzled the group with her smile again. "Through hard work and perseverance, they made it into the baking empire it is today."

"Who runs it now?" Pricilla Rose, or Pri for short, had raised her hand but asked the question before being called on.

"Mr. Brimwell," Claire replied.

"Why, that would make him almost a hundred years old," Pri said, surprised.

"Silly me," Claire chuckled. "Please forgive me, I meant to say his grandson, B.J. Brimwell, who met you at the front door. He didn't look quite 100, did he?" Heads bobbed in understanding, and a few boys even laughed at the dull joke.

More facts were mentioned, and the tour kept moving. Mr. West told them they would have a paper due concerning their tour, and Mina needed an A on this paper, badly. Sometime during the lecture on the usefulness of different sugars in the chocolate process, Mr. West had become separated from the tour group, but only Mina seemed to notice their ward's absence.

Claire seemed to enjoy the extra attention from the boys, particularly Brody, and did nothing to discourage them. The tour went through the stockroom, the drying room, and the mixing rooms. Every room looked the same, sterile and depressing, the workers even more so in their drab white coats, shower caps, and listless, droning movements. The expression on every one of the workers' faces was the same: blank.

Mina noticed that many of the students were becoming bored, and more than a few could be seen trying to stifle their yawns, so as not to upset their guide. Mina felt her eyes start to go heavy, as if she hadn't slept in days.

Slowly the atmosphere of the tour changed. Mina hardly noticed when the steady stream of facts slowed significantly and Claire's voice no longer echoed loudly enough to reach the back of the room. In fact, Claire had hardly spoken above a whisper for the last five minutes. The rest of the class became incidental, as the tour now seemed to only consist of one VIP—Brody.

Claire would lean in and gently put her hand on his shoulder to direct him if he was turning the wrong way. She would whisper a comment that only he seemed to hear. Everything about the small movements and encounters between the two seemed odd, out of place. Claire stopped walking to listen to a comment that Brody made, turned her head coyly to the side, and giggled. Actually giggled. Now Mina wished that she wasn't at the back of the group so she could hear what was said. But someone obviously did overhear; Savannah moved in for the kill.

Savannah flipped her blonde hair and physically stepped between Claire and Brody, her nose turned up in challenge. "Excuse me. Perhaps you could stop paying so much attention to my boyfriend so we can actually hear you in the back." Claire's eyes turned dark as Brody grabbed her elbow and turned on her.

"You have GOT to be kidding, Savannah. Are you trying to embarrass me?"

"Are you? When's the last time you were so interested in a stupid bread barn?"

"Oh, come on. Really, you want to do this now?"

"Do what now?" she asked coldly.

Brody's voice grew louder. Everyone stopped talking to listen in to what was sure to be the biggest argument of the semester, and they were going to witness it firsthand.

"It's over between us. I'm sick of you. I'm sick of your jealousy and your childish ways. It's time for you to grow up!" Brody looked feverish and tense. Sweat beaded off his forehead.

Savannah's eyes glistened with tears, and her cherry-glossed lip started to tremble. "You don't mean that. Yesterday you told me…"

"Well, that was yesterday and this is today. Don't you get it? You're too much of a baby." The words left Brody's mouth, but they seemed awkward and forced. Savannah turned and ran back down the hallway toward the bathrooms. Pri dutifully ran after her.

Claire turned to the group and smiled brightly. "Well, now that that embarrassing scene is over with, let's be on our way, shall we?" Her smile was so blindingly bright that it was almost painful look at.

Did no one else seem to notice the effect the bewitching tour guide was having on Brody and the boys? Apparently not. The girls were so upset by the breakup that they were no longer paying attention to the tour, instead whispering among themselves excitedly about sudden availability of the hottest guy in school. No one ever could hold a grudge against Brody Carmichael.

Nan nudged Mina and motioned to the group of girls with her chin. "I told you that everyone loves gossip. I've already been texted by three different people who aren't even here that Brody and Savannah broke up." Nan frowned, looking at one of the texts, and her fingers flew over the touchpad. "No, that's not right. I was here. I saw it." Nan began murmuring to herself as she tried to fix whatever new rumor was now flying through their high school ten miles away.

Claire finally led the tour group to the third floor and was allowing the kids to walk the railed catwalk over the production floor. By now, many of the students had become bored and started laughing and horsing around. It seemed that whatever love spell that once charmed them had worn off, except for one hypnotized Brody. His movements become slower, and he was transfixed by Claire's every movement.

Mina watched as Claire's hand stroked Brody's bicep in a demure manner. Warning bells went off in her head that something was definitely wrong. A tingling began in her hands and spread throughout her body and up her spine like an electric current. Jumping, Mina looked around and behind her for a source of static electricity, but no one was near her.

Another intense feeling of wrongness overcame her, and she felt compelled to move forward and interfere. She didn't want to make a spectacle like Savannah, but she had to break whatever spell Claire had over Brody. Gathering her courage, Mina moved forward, unsure of exactly what she was going to do. The tingling sensation was almost overwhelming.

Someone bumped her from behind, and she lost her grip on her notebook and chewed-up pencil, which launched from her hand to land at the feet of Steven and Frank, deep in some argument over a video game. She watched as the pencil rolled right in front of Steven's foot, wincing when the foot came down and he slipped on the pencil. Steven flailed his arms dramatically, causing a domino effect as he lost his balance and pitched forward into Frank.

Frank, caught off guard, tried to catch his friend but ended up slamming backward into Mina, Claire, and Brody. Mina caught her balance, but Claire's heel snagged in the catwalk, and she stumbled headlong into Brody, pushing him toward the railing. The rickety walkway shifted under the weight, causing everyone to lurch to the right.

The sudden jostling woke Brody from his hypnotic state. She saw his sudden confusion, followed by shock as the catwalk tilted again. He stumbled backward; his arms flailed widely as he reached for a hand railing and missed. His blue eyes filled with terror as he fell backward over the safety rail.

CHAPTER 2

Screams of horror reverberated off the walls. Adrenaline took over as Mina lunged for Brody, missing his body entirely but grabbing the shoulder strap of his black Jansport backpack. She had done it without thinking, even though she wasn't very strong, and now she gritted her teeth as she slammed into the railing, causing her to cry out in pain. There was a moment of suspended animation when she thought she had him and they were safe, but then her feet slowly lost contact with the floor. Screaming, she started moving upward and over, her feet dangling uselessly. She was going to go over the railing with him.

Suddenly, hands grabbed her around the waist, anchoring her. Both her and Brody's downward momentum stopped with a jolt and a loud rip. She kept a death grip on the backpack strap and felt pain shoot up through both arms.

Brody had one arm through the other strap; it had slid down to his elbow. Reaching up, he used his other hand to hold on to get a firmer grip. He stared upward, a panicked look on his face, the catwalk still swaying precariously.

"Don't worry! I've got you, Brody." Mina tried to sound comforting, even though her muscles burned and her arms shook from the strain of holding onto someone twice her weight.

"And I've got you." Nan's voice was muffled from exertion. She was the one who had kept Mina from going over. Other students began to aid in the rescue. Steven and

Frank reached over to grab the backpack, helping to relieve the burden of Brody's weight. They helped pull him up to where Brody was able to grab onto the lower safety bar.

Their own safety set aside, a few students lay on their stomachs and knees to reach through the rails to grab onto Brody as he slowly pulled his own weight up to where his feet could find purchase on the catwalk.

Mina felt like she couldn't breathe until Brody had stepped back over the railing and was safe. Once he was out of danger, she fell to her knees on the diamond-shaped grating, ignoring the painful prods as she was overcome with a feeling of intense relief. Brody's backpack was dumped on the floor next to her. He leaned down to talk to Mina, but Steven and Frank pulled him away in excitement. Mina looked at the ripped backpack and had to blink twice to see if she was delusional. The rip she had heard was Brody's backpack ripping, and it was in the exact same place and size as the hole in her backpack from this morning. Only he could probably afford to buy a new one.

Even though Brody was safe, Mina felt like she wasn't. She felt as if she were being smothered. As if some unseen force was watching her, judging her, and the feeling was becoming unbearably strong. With all the kids' eyes on her, she felt trapped.

Even Claire looked rattled and scared, her blonde hair disheveled, her safety hat gone. Limping, she tried to stand and gain control of the students, who were celebrating, hugging, and crying. Several students slapped Mina's back.

"That was awesome!"

"I can't believe you acted to so quickly!"

"You saved his life."

"Way to go, Grimes!"

"I think it's time we went outside," Claire said, her eyes downcast in shame. Everyone followed her to the closest emergency exit and down the steps to a side door that led outside. The bright sunlight touching the students' faces seemed to burn away the weary fog that had previously overtaken them.

Mina felt her unease slightly diminish once she was a good distance away from the building, but it didn't leave entirely.

They took the long way and walked around the side of the bakery until they came to the front entrance and the bus. Mr. West was there, along with Mr. Brimwell. For an irresponsible chaperone, Mr. West was quick to see that there was a problem. He read the agitation on Claire's face and instantly became alert.

"What happened? What's wrong?" he asked.

Claire spoke up, her face red with embarrassment. "There was an unfortunate accident on the catwalk."

Mr. West's eyes went wide in fear. His bald head looked like a pendulum as he began swinging it back and forth, trying to take a head count of his pack of unruly students.

"Yeah, Brody almost died!" Steven blurted out. Savannah let out a high-pitched squeak of alarm.

"He fell backward off the catwalk, but Grimes…I mean, Mina, saved him!" Frank yelled.

Nothing else could be heard over the roar of voices as everyone spoke up at once, trying to relay their own version of the death-defying story. Mina was uncomfortable with all the staring, so she tried to maneuver to the outside of the crowd and duck behind Nan, who was no longer preoccupied with her phone.

Mr. Brimwell paled and looked to Claire. "Is this true? How could you have let this happen?"

Claire pinched her lips together angrily. "It wasn't my fault. They were messing around on the catwalk, and a support cinch failed."

Mina's stomach dropped, and she felt sick. None of them knew the real reason. None of this would have happened if she hadn't dropped her chewed-up number-two pencil. This whole mess started because of how clumsy she was and her inherent bad luck. It was another epic disaster to add to the list in her sock drawer at home. She felt so disheartened.

"You let these kids on the catwalk?" Mr. Brimwell accused her. His round face turned red like a tomato with anger, but that didn't dissuade Claire.

"Why wouldn't I? I've been taking people on the catwalk for years, and it's never bothered you before. I've always ended tours there."

They drew closer together, and the heated argument became indecipherable amongst the growing babble of Mina's classmates. Mr. West's head seemed to be shaking in disbelief, and he kept looking over at Mina skeptically. She didn't blame him. She could hardly believe her own actions.

Mina blushed as he looked past Savannah and over the heads of the students, searching for something or someone. She saw Brody spot her among the crowd and start to move in her direction. She tensed. She couldn't imagine him thanking her for such an embarrassing stunt, especially in front of twenty students with cell phones. She was likely to say something dumb and make a fool of herself.

Mina couldn't look away as he maneuvered around the sympathetic girls to reach her. He was only feet away when Savannah cried his name and caught his attention. Brody and

Mina both turned to find her running toward him, impossibly blonde hair swinging behind her as she ran into his arms. "Are you okay?" she asked hesitantly, unsure of her reception. Mina hoped he'd blow her off, but to her surprise he cradled her in an enormous hug.

"Brody, I'm so sorry!" Savannah said when they'd pulled apart. Could she really be so oblivious to the audience around them? "I'm sorry about how I acted in the factory. You're right—I do need to grow up, and I promise to never embarrass you like that again." Her bottom lip actually trembled.

"Savannah, what are you talking about? This wasn't your fault."

"No, not that. Our argument. I've done a lot of thinking and…"

"What argument?" Brody said, sounding frustrated. Mina heard stunned whispers throughout the crowd. "Savannah, I almost died. Can we talk about this some other time?"

"Wait… You don't remember?"

"Truthfully this whole morning is kind of a haze. I'm really not feeling well…maybe I should just go home."

Hope filled Savannah's face, her trembles ceasing when she realized Brody didn't remember their breakup. "You're right, Brody. Let's get you home." She clutched his arm possessively and led him toward the bus and a panicked Mr. West.

"Brody, my boy, I hope your family doesn't think it was negligence on my part. I got called away on an important phone call." Mr. West placed his hand on Brody's shoulder and gave a wary glance toward Mr. Brimwell. Turning toward the rest of the students, he called out in the tone that only a teacher can do, "All right students, lets load up."

Mina filed behind Nan and Pri, and waited to board the bus. She watched as the unsteady Brody was led up the steps onto the bus with the help of Savannah.

"Well, I guess that was the shortest breakup in history," Pri mumbled.

"Don't be too sure about that," Nan said, thoughtfully glancing at Brody.

Mina watched him take a window seat and stare balefully out it in her direction. He seemed to be staring at her! Mina immediately looked at the ground, but when she looked back up, she still had his gaze. It was a tad uncomfortable.

"I mean, I don't even know what he sees in her," Pri continued.

"Don't worry, Pri. I have a feeling that the makeup is only temporary."

As Mina boarded the bus, students began clapping and calling her name, reaching out to give her high-fives and congratulate her on her heroic act. Except for one, who was still staring out the window. She felt like she was going to be sick; her guilt was making her a nervous wreck. Should she apologize to Brody? That would mean she would have to go up to him and actually speak to the world's most handsome boy, who didn't seem eager to talk to her. Definitely not. Maybe she could slip him a note? That wouldn't do. What if his family sued hers? Yep, Mina was definitely going to puke.

Keeping her head down, Mina hastily made her way to the back of the bus and slid down as far as she could into her seat in an attempt to hide. Nan slid in next to her.

"Kinda nice to be sitting next to a celebrity." Nan laughed.

"No, it's not. It's horrible," Mina said. "You were wrong. I don't want to be popular."

"Maybe I should get your autograph and sell it on eBay. Or better yet, I could auction off your old English papers. I wonder how much money I would get for a D-plus?" Mina was terrified at the prospect. "Then I could buy that new handbag I wanted," Nan said.

"I hope you choke on the handbag," Mina shot back.

Nan chuckled, but she quit making ribs at Mina's expense. She leaned out the bus aisle to take a peek. Sure enough, everyone was still looking toward her, pointing and whispering in her direction. Sighing in regret, she leaned back dramatically and drummed her fingers on her thighs.

"Aren't you going to tweet this?" Mina said, noticing the lack of an electronic accessory in Nan's hands. "I thought for sure you would have taken fifty photos by now."

"Can't," Nan sighed wistfully.

"Why not?"

"I don't have my iPhone anymore."

"What happened?"

"I threw it off the catwalk as soon as I saw you were in trouble. I mean, come on, it was either hold on to my stupid phone or save my best friend's life," she said, holding out her hands and weighing imaginary items. "Duh! Not a tough decision."

Mina reached over and hugged Nan as tightly as she could. She knew how much Nan's life revolved around that stupid phone, and her friend did help save her.

Nan made gagging noises as she squeezed harder and harder. "Gee, let go, let go."

"Thank you, Nan." Mina smiled.

"Yeah, yeah, I know. You're indebted to me for life. You're my eternal slave and must sacrifice yourself to save me now. Blah, blah, blah." Nan waved her hands in the air like it was nothing.

Mina and Nan sat back down in their seats and listened to the harmony of a busload of students texting, talking, and playing games on their cell phones. The chiming noise was a constant reminder of Nan's sacrifice.

"Nan?" Mina began, getting ready to apologize again.

"Don't!" Nan snapped, holding her pink polished finger up to silence any more words. "I already regret it."

Mina laughed.

CHAPTER 3

Mina hadn't told her mother what happened at Babushka's, knowing exactly how she would react. Sara was an extremely overprotective mother, far beyond what seemed normal or even sane. Anytime a crazy unexplained accident happened to Mina, Sara would pick up the family and move, no questions asked. Mina wasn't really sure why.

In first grade, Mina took a trip to the zoo and was overcome with anxiety as all the animals in the petting zoo started following her around. They had moved the following week.

In fourth grade, Mina's garden-variety science project produced two car-sized pumpkins overnight. They moved the next day.

In seventh grade during Home-Ec., Mina kept falling asleep during her knitting projects. Sara told the school it was mono, and their family was packed by the time Mina got home.

Mina knew that what had happened yesterday was worse than any of her other unpleasant accidents, which was why she kept the list. She hoped to one day find hidden a link between these disasters and figure out what made her mother want to move.

For now she was lucky that her mother wasn't close to any of the moms from school. If she were, Mina might already have found their small apartment packed up in boxes and a moving truck in the alley.

"Mina?" Sara peeked her head into her daughter's room, the door almost immediately stopped by the piles of teenage debris. When Mina didn't answer, Sara braved the obstacle course of clothes and magazines and walked into her daughter's dark room to open the blinds and window.

"Ahhhh, MOM!" Mina answered, throwing the comforter back over her head to protect herself from the onslaught of fresh air and light, both of which were toxic to a very sleepy teenager. Grumbling, she curled up under the covers and tried to ignore her mother's movements throughout her room. All she wanted was to lie in bed comatose for another few hours as she gathered strength to face another day at school. Was that too much to ask? When Sara stubbed her toe on an unidentified object, she let out a gasp of pain but held back any forthcoming remarks. Mina bit her lip guiltily under the covers, knowing she really needed to clean up her room. She was grateful that her mother never harangued her about it.

"We're leaving now. I have to pick up a few things before taking Charlie to school. I'll be late coming home after I drop off a packet at the Carmichaels' residence. Be home for dinner, okay?"

"Wait! The Carmichaels? No way!" Mina shrieked, sitting up in bed and throwing the comforter behind her. "I mean, don't they have live-in maids? Why would they want to employ another company?" Mina knew that whatever happened, she could not let her mother go to the Carmichaels'. What if they told her mother about what happened at the bakery? What if they tried to thank Sara? Or worse, what if her mother became the Carmichaels' *maid*. No. Mina could not let that happen.

"Well, maybe they heard what a great job we do and want to hire the best. We definitely could use the extra money." Sara looked at the piles of clothes and sighed wearily.

"What if I do it?" Mina shot out without thinking.

"Do what, honey?" Sara nudged a pair of dirty socks with her shoe over to what she assumed was a dirty clothes pile.

Mina had to think fast. "I lent Brody my notes, so I have to go over there today anyhow. So give me the Happy Maids packet, and I'll drop it off for Mrs. Carmichael."

Sara thought about it. "Well, that would work, because then I wouldn't be late to the Browns'. Why, thank you, Mina." Sara smiled.

Mina tried and failed to return her mother's smile when she realized the full implications of what she'd volunteered to do. Mina was an idiot.

Sara put the packet on the kitchen table, and Mina watched as she and her younger brother, wearing a Superman cape, headed out the door. Mina ran back to her bedroom, grabbed a purple pillow off her bed, and screamed into it, dancing around the room.

Green movement captured Mina's attention, and she froze when she realized that her mother had opened her window and blinds. Mrs. Orn, the eighty-year-old cat lady from the building next door, was watching her with one eyebrow fully raised. She'd happened to be watering her window box full of daisies when Mina made her dancing debut, and was now likely drowning them.

"Sorry, Mrs. Orn," Mina called, and dashed to the ledge to close the window and blinds.

Looking at the clock, Mina was glad to see that she had woken up with plenty of time to take a shower. Grabbing her robe, she flung it over the top shower bar and began to work on the infinite twists and turns of the shower spigots. It was easier to crack a double combination safe than it was to coax hot water out of these ancient pipes. Mina said a quick prayer to the god of plumbing and bathroom fixtures and, after a few spurts of murky brown water, hot water eventually began to rain down.

After a quick and refreshing shower, she donned her blue terry bathrobe and slippers and pulled on the ancient porcelain bathroom door. She must not have prayed hard enough to the god of bathroom fixtures, because the bathroom door handle came off in her hands.

"NO…No…no…no. This can't be happening!" Mina pounded frantically on the door and called for help before remembering her mother and brother had left early. Mina desperately tried to reattach the door handle, but all she succeeded in doing was pushing the other one out the other side.

Mina bit back a scream of frustration. Getting on her knees, she tried to look through the bathroom hole and find out what sort of lock it was. After assessing the situation, Mina discovered she had no clue what it was or how to get out. Frantically, she began to pull out drawers and open cupboards to look for something she could jam into the hole and turn the door. She tried several different things: her mother's tweezers, and her hairbrush, which was too thick. She had nearly given up her search when finally her eyes fell on the toothbrush holder.

Would it work? Should she try? Grabbing the fattest toothbrush, which happened to be Charlie's, Mina inserted it handle first and gave it a few turns. It pulled on the lock a bit, but not enough to release the catch. Opening up another drawer, Mina grabbed a nail file and inserted it between the door frame and the catch. If she could budge the latch enough to push the nail file through, she'd be free.

For the next few minutes she pushed the file against the catch, carefully twisting the toothbrush back and forth until eventually she felt the door slide open in response.

Mina could almost have cried in relief. Just another reason to talk to her mother about getting a cell phone. But this latest debacle had made her late for school. Grabbing a violet zippered hoodie, Mina ran out the door and across the lawn, having to double back only once to grab the Happy Maids packet from the kitchen table.

After pedaling for two blocks on her bicycle, Mina heard a slight mewing noise. Looking down, she saw an orange tabby cat keeping pace just to her right. Mina swerved a few feet to the right to avoid the cat and almost ran over a large dog that was now on the left of her bike.

"Yikes!" Mina stood up and tried to pedal harder to outdistance the animals, but after a few more labored breaths, she looked behind her and saw they were still there.

"Go away! Shoo!" Mina was worried that the dog and cat would continue to follow her and get hit by a car. They sped up and seemed to be chasing Mina. Who would have thought a dog and cat together would be chasing her on her bike?

A loud screech and the large colorful object flying toward her head was the only warning that Mina had of a rooster propelling himself from a nearby fence. Ducking, Mina swerved and almost lost control of the bike.

"What the…?" This was the oddest thing that had happened to Mina in a while. She turned her head to see the rooster land behind her next to the dog and cat, and it seemed to join in on the chase.

Turning her head, Mina had only a split second to register that there was a large animal directly in her path, and slammed on her brakes. Too late. Mina lost control and flew headlong over the handlebars of her bike to land crumpled on the sidewalk. In that instant, Mina recognized the animal that caused her wreck, but she couldn't believe it. It was a donkey, in the middle of town. And was it wearing a hat?

***

Shivering and sore because of her wet hair and skinned hands, Mina rode slowly the rest of the way to school. She decided today was turning into another epic disaster. When she hit the sidewalk, she must have blacked out for a split second. Either that or she was hallucinating, because when she dusted off her hands and looked around, there was no sign of the donkey, rooster, dog, or cat. There was no evidence that they were ever there. Mina ran up and down the block looking for the donkey, but with no success. Maybe it wasn't a donkey. Maybe it was another large dog? She didn't even bother pulling up to the bike rack, but threw her bike on the ground, her feet pounding the pavement as she ran up the stairs and into school.

Mina glanced at her watch; she was five minutes late for class. Keeping her head down, she tried to walk as fast and as quietly as she could, hoping to avoid the hall monitors. Maybe if she pleaded hard enough with her first-hour teacher, she would have pity and avoid writing a tardy slip. Yeah, right.

Her teacher, Mrs. Porter, had her back to the door and was writing on the whiteboard, so Mina slipped into the classroom and tried to nonchalantly slide into her desk next to Nan. Mina took a quick peek at the rigid spine of Mrs. Porter, noticing that the teacher never turned or made any movement to acknowledge her late entrance. She turned slightly and began to shuffle some papers around on her desk; she didn't even glance Mina's way. Mina was just about to breathe a sigh of relief when Mrs. Porter walked over and dropped a tardy slip on her desk, with Mina's name written in perfect penmanship across on the top.

She never even saw her teacher fill out the form. Mina took the yellow slip of paper between her shaking fingers and looked toward Mrs. Porter's desk in confusion.

Mrs. Porter's thin pale lips tightened into what could only be described as an inhuman smile. "I find that it saves time if I fill out your tardy slips in advance, Ms. Grime. It's less of a distraction for the class, and you seem to be the only one that has this peculiar problem." She held up a stack of the small carbon-copy yellow forms and spread them so everyone could see her name printed on the next five tardy slips. "As you can see, you haven't disappointed me yet." Her eyes tried to crinkle as she laughed, but everything looked strange and awkward on her. She was so old that the whites of her eyes were no longer white but a pasty gray. Her teeth looked like faded yellow parchment, and her clothes seemed to have come from the 1950s.

Everything about Mrs. Porter was a throwback to some other era and time. Even the antique candy bowl that sat on her desk with ancient, uneaten candy corn seemed forlorn and out of place amongst the high-tech gadgetry of the classroom.

Mrs. Porter had been with the school since it first opened and refused to retire, which was why she only taught homeroom or study hall. While other teachers had moved onto video chat guest speakers and live televised distant learning, her teaching methods were so far outdated that she made fuzzy 70s-era VHS tapes seem modern. Mina guessed she had never so much as touched a computer. But there was one thing that Mrs. Porter did and did well, and that was discipline. She prided herself on handing out the most detention slips and tardy notices, explaining that the other teachers had gone soft.

Mina shrank into her seat, crumpling the tardy notice and stuffing it into her pocket. It wasn't fair that she was always late. Most of the time it was out of her control. Biting her lip, she tried to study her algebra notes when a persistent foot kept nudging her Converse. Mina looked up into the excited eyes of Nan, who was being careful to mouth her words so as not to be overheard.

"Have you heard? There's an assembly. About you," she mouthed.

"What?" Mina said audibly. Quickly she ducked her head and buried it in her notebook, just as Mrs. Porter swung around at the noise. The woman might be old, but she had hearing like a bat. Mina pretended to scribble in her book, and out of the corner of her eye she watched as Nan pursed her lips and tapped her pencil on her book as if solving a complicated problem. Mrs. Porter scanned the room, then turned her back and continued her writing.

Nan blew out a breath of air that made her bangs float in the air before resting nonchalantly on her cheek. Her hair always looked effortless. She raised her eyebrow at Mina as if waiting for a response. Mina glanced at the back of her teacher and shook her head.

Nan scribbled in her notebook and flipped up the edge so Mina could see what she'd written. *News reporters, photographers, media in the gym.*

Mina's brows furrowed in confusion. "Why?" she mouthed quietly this time.

Nan gave an exasperated head bob that could only mean one word, "duh," and began scribbling in her notebook. This time only three words appeared.

You and Brody!

Mina's head began to shake back and forth in disbelief. This was exactly the kind of debacle she was afraid would happen. What if her mom found out and made them move?

Nan widened her eyes, nodding slowly in affirmation. If someone else had looked at Mina and Nan right then, they would have seen two bobble heads at war.

Nan stopped nodding, and scribbled in her notebook and held it for Mina to read. *Promise me that I get an insider's scoop.*

Mina rolled her eyes but whispered, "Fine."

Nan used her hand to cross her heart. Mina smiled and did the same, the whole time shaking in her shoes. With a few more quick notes, Mina was able to discern what she had missed by being late that morning. The assembly would be held at second period in the gym.

What was supposed to be a glorifying rally seemed more like an executioner's sentence. Why couldn't she be more like other kids and enjoy these things? Instead, she was terrified and tried to think of ways to escape. Maybe she could feign sickness and go home. One look at Mrs. Porter made Mina realize it'd never work. She would make her tough it out or maybe go so far as to escort her to the nurse's office herself. Any other period, and she could come up with some excuse and slip out unnoticed. But not this one. Her only other option would be to leave as soon as the bell rang.

The forty-five-minute class seemed to drag on, and Mina gave up trying to study for her algebra class. Her eyes began to water from staring at the clock for so long. With only one minute left, Mina grabbed her bag and was moving toward the door one second before the bell sounded.

Yes! Mina escaped the room, and had just turned right down the hallway and toward the exit when she walked into Principal Hame.

"Ah, Mina! Just the person we were looking for. Please come with me." His heavy hand on her shoulder felt like a manacle snapping around her neck. She watched someone exit the school doors, and the sound of them closing reverberated in her ears. Mina winced.

"Um, Principal Hame, I'm not feeling well this morning, and I think it would be beneficial if I went home immediately." She tried to slump her shoulders and look sick.

"You can't leave now. We have something very special planned for you." He brushed off her terrible acting and shuffled toward the office, pulling her alongside him. In the background, Mina heard the noise of lockers being shut and the excitement of students moving toward the gym. They loved any excuse to skip class.

Principal Hame guided Mina into his office and had her sit in one of the chairs facing his desk. His office was decorated with pigs, and lots of them. Ceramic pigs, plastic bobble heads, stuffed pigs, even a Hog Heaven monthly calendar. Everywhere you looked there were pigs, mostly because his secretary gifted him with a pig decoration for every occasion. Mina knew she was a lost cause for tardiness when she began naming the pigs. She stared dejectedly at a ceramic pig with a red polka dot tie perched on Principal Hame's desk. This one she named *Lucky* because he was the least stupid-looking of the collection.

Principal Hame slumped into his chair and had a moment of awkwardness as his chair slid back three feet from the desk.

After a few grunts and pushes, he maneuvered the chair back to the desk. Mina did her best to keep a straight face. "As you may have heard, Channel 6 and the *Herald Stadium* are here to do an interview with you about your heroic efforts yesterday. What I need to know, Mina, is whether you love your school."

"I don't understand, Principal Hame."

Principal Hame coughed. "Well, Mina, what I should be asking is maybe how much you like your fellow students and friends, like Nan Taylor. It would be a shame if our school lost funding and had to cut programs because of bad publicity."

"How could this be bad publicity? I'm not sure I understand your question. Of course I love this school. I'm just terrified of giving an interview and would really prefer not to. So if you could find a way out for me, that would be incredible."

"Mina, you have to do the interview. I just want to make sure that you don't place blame on Mr. West for the incident that happened at Babushka's. If it was publicized that he wasn't there when the accident occurred, it could be seen as negligence, and we could lose our most valued supporters and be forced to cut funding or even, God forbid, fire Mr. West. The Carmichaels have a lot of powerful friends. I need to know whether you think Mr. West is to blame for the accident."

Mina was at a loss for words. "Of course not! He wasn't the one to blame. It was my—no one's fault. Just an accident." Mina had almost admitted the truth. How could she place blame on an absent teacher when she knew that even if Mr. West was there, the same events would have unfolded with the same outcome? It was just her bad luck that followed her everywhere.

Principal Hame smiled brightly. "Excellent! Glad to hear it. Well, we'd better get you to the gym." He stood up and ushered Mina out the door, following close on her heels.

"No, really, I'm not feeling that well and would rather go home," Mina pleaded. In retrospect, she wished she had used the time in his office to try to blackmail him into letting her go home, but it was too late now.

Again Principal Hame ignored her, "Make sure you tell the reporters how much you love our school. We would love to get a new pool installed, you know. Good publicity equals good funding."

"But I…"

"Now's your time to shine, Ms. Grime. Do your school proud." Principal Hame escorted Mina down the corridor, and before she knew it, she was through the doors into the gym.

"THERE SHE IS!" Nan yelled, waving at the reporters while pointing to Mina.

Yep, Mina thought to herself, she was definitely going to kill Nan.

Principal Hame sauntered proudly to the center and took the mic from Vice Principal Merris. "And here she is: Kennedy High School's own real-life heroine. Wilhelmina Grime!" He started clapping into the microphone, which caused a chain reaction amongst the whole student body.

Mrs. Colbert, the music teacher, came forward and gently led a nervous Mina to the half-court line in the gym. Principal Hame heartily slapped her back as if she were a linebacker instead of a five-foot-four girl. Mina had just choked back a snappy retort when a bright flashing light blinded her. Photographers appeared from nowhere. The band started playing the school theme song, and the whole student body began stomping on the bleachers.

No longer was the air filled with cries of "Slimy Grimy," "Loser," or "Nerd," but her name. The students were chanting her full and much-hated, antiquated name, Wilhelmina Grimes— everyone except for one tall, good-looking boy. Mina felt her heart sink when she saw that Brody Carmichael wasn't standing with the other students, chanting or cheering for her. He was sitting in the front row, chewing on his lip. Just sitting and staring at her, brows furrowed, leaning forward to see her over the crowd. She couldn't even begin to discern the emotions on his face.

"Mina, tell us what happened at Babushka's Bakery the day you saved the Carmichaels' son from certain death?" The reporter from the Channel 6 news station thrust a microphone in front of Mina's face. Another flash from the *Herald Stadium* newspaper photographer caught her off guard, making her dizzy. But that wasn't what irritated Mina, it was the reporter's poor choice of words.

"He has a name," Mina shot back, furious that the reporter would refer to Brody as the Carmichaels' son, and not by his name. She thought he deserved better.

"Of course he does," the reporter countered. "Are you going to answer the question?"

"Not until you rephrase your question."

"Now, Mina," Principal Hame interjected. "Now's not the time to argue semantics. They are doing a lovely story on our school and on you because of what happened yesterday. It will be good publicity and may even help us get grants for our library."

"Of all the self-centered, hare-brained…" Mina muttered under her breath, knowing that no one outside of the few feet around them could hear them over the band. What a game the principal was playing; earlier he'd mentioned a pool, and now it was a library.

"Ah ah ah. Now remember, it's for the good of the school," Principal Hame chided.

"Fine! There was some rough-housing on the catwalk, and someone fell into BRODY CARMICHAEL." Mina spoke his name loudly. "And he fell over the safety railing."

"And you saved him?" the reporter asked. Did she detect a note of sarcasm in his voice?

"Yeah, I guess I did. I wasn't thinking, I just reacted. I grabbed for him and got his backpack. I started to go over the railing, too, except that Nan..." Mina pointed to her friend, who was screaming in the bleachers, "grabbed me and saved both of us. Nan Taylor is the real hero of the story, not me. She even sacrificed her iPhone in the attempt to save us." As soon as Mina directed the attention to Nan, the reporter and her flock of photographers moved on and up the bleachers toward a surprised Nan.

"That was a brave thing you did," Mrs. Colbert leaned in and whispered over her shoulder.

Mina shrugged. "I didn't do anything special. Only did what anyone else in my situation would have done."

"I'm sure that's not the case, but you can keep telling yourself that if it helps you sleep better." Mrs. Colbert smiled knowingly. Her short spiky hair and blue-colored, wing-tipped glasses gave her an approachable edge, though her quips and riddles often left Mina more confused than enlightened.

"Why are they not interviewing Brody? I thought for sure they would be all over him." Mina glanced over her shoulder to see a furious Brody glaring in her direction again. She swallowed nervously.

"They can't. The Carmichael family has forbidden the newspapers from harassing their son."

"But I thought no one could silence the media." Mina looked back up toward where Brody was now sitting. Not a single photographer bothered him. Another flash of light in Mina's direction, and she was seeing stars again.

"That's what they want you to think, but the biggest pocketbook speaks loudest." She grinned, causing her cheek to dimple. "They allow their own names, photos, and stories to be printed, but the Carmichaels control all publicity regarding their son." Mrs. Colbert walked away to settle down Steve and Frank, who had taken their shirts off and were waving them above their heads, trying to get on the news.

Through the next hour Mina stayed in the gym, retelling the same story over and over. Just when she didn't think it could get any more humiliating, it did, because by lunchtime she was on YouTube.

"That was exciting!" Nan gushed as she pushed her tray along the lunch line. She was wearing another black shirt, this time dedicated to a certain sparkly vampire. She picked up an apple, turkey sandwich, and a pink frosted cupcake from the line and swiped her lunch card through the electronic reader.

Mina was too stressed to eat. She grabbed chocolate milk from the cooler and paid, following Nan to their favorite table by the window. They were stopped three times by students wanting pictures and autographs.

"I bet your followers have doubled," Mina commented as Nan waved cheerily at the group of freshmen, who kept pointing and whispering.

"Tripled! But who's counting?" She smiled. Obviously, Nan was.

Mina shook her milk, and began to think about her string of bad luck getting to school.

"What's with the scowl?" said Nan.

"You wouldn't believe the morning I had."

"I know, I was here, remember."

"No, I'm talking about before I even got to school." Mina began to relay the entire morning's events, even up to Principal Hame's office, but Nan only heard one thing.

"WHAT!" she squealed, kicking Mina excitedly under the table. "Are you serious? You get to go to Brody Carmichael's house?"

"Nan, you're not listening. Something strange is going on. I think I'm going crazy." She looked out the window and could see the sky beginning to turn green, a sure sign that a storm was coming.

"You bet you are. I can't believe you didn't tell me about the Carmichaels as soon as you saw me."

"You're missing the point."

"No, I heard it. You're being terrorized by strange domestic animals. I'll buy you some repellent."

"Don't forget the donkey. I don't know if I would call that a domestic animal. What do you make of that?"

"You said yourself it could have been a large dog. But do you hear yourself? *You* are going to Brody's house. You've had a crush on him for two years. When were you going to tell me?"

"I'm telling you now!"

"Are you excited?" Nan leaned in eagerly, her hands likely itching for her iPhone.

"Not really, because I don't really plan on going. I was hoping you would go for me." Mina slid the blue folder with the sticker of the Happy Maids logo across the table to Nan.

Nan looked at the folder in shock and slid it back. "Uh, no! This is your dreamy stalker moment, not mine. You do it."

"I can't, Nan. I just can't." Mina looked at Nan and pleaded silently. "I'm not ready to talk to him."

Nan peeled the paper from around her cupcake and gave it a bite. "If you can't talk to him now, after you saved his life, you're never going to talk to him. Besides I have a good feeling about this. Trust me."

Mina wished she did trust Nan. But every time Nan said those two words, Mina ended up in trouble.

"So how's Charlie?" Nan said, changing the subject.

"He's doing well. He really likes the new school." Mina knew why her friend was trying to change the subject, but she let her get away with it.

"Do they think they can get him to talk?" Nan asked, swiping her finger through the frosting on her cupcake. Mina's brother Charlie was born shortly after their father died, and even though the doctors could find nothing wrong with him, he never spoke.

"They hope so. They seem to think it's because he was in the womb when Dad died, that he absorbed some of Mom's post-traumatic depression or something."

"What do you think?" Nan asked, licking the rest of the frosting from her fingers.

"I think Charlie doesn't speak because he doesn't need to."

"You still think he will just one day awake from whatever silent spell he's under and begin talking, like some sort of fairy tale?"

"Nan, you know I don't believe in fairy tales." As soon as the words left Mina's mouth, a crash of thunder shook the cafeteria, and the lights flickered on and off. Girls screamed in

41

fright, and the boys laughed out loud, pointing fingers and trying to re-scare some of the girls.

"Whoa…freaky!" Nan bobbed her head and looked around in wonder. "That was cool." They looked out across the campus and could see the wind begin to pick up, but no visible rain yet.

"It's just a storm," Mina tried to answer carelessly. But her heart was racing with adrenaline. When it finally settled, Mina went on, "But, Nan, if I believed in fairy tales, then wouldn't there have to be a dashing prince to save me from my pathetic life?"

"Well, you know," Nan began to counter….

"Forget it. There are no happily-ever-afters. Look at my mom—she's a maid, for crying out loud, a widowed mother with two children. Where's her happy ending?" Mina opened her chocolate milk and took a drink. "There are no such things as fairy tales." Another crash of thunder shook the metal roof of the ceiling, causing Mina to spill chocolate milk down her violet jacket. A downpour of rain followed a second after, pinging loudly on the roof.

"Do you see what I mean?" Mina pulled her wet hoodie away from her body as she tried to wipe up the mess with a wad of napkins. "I'm cursed to be a loser forever."

"You know, Mina," Nan said thoughtfully as she grabbed napkins that didn't have frosting on them to help her friend. "Not every tale has a happy ending. In fact, many of them are grim."

CHAPTER 4

Mina couldn't believe she was doing this. The only reason she'd decided to go through with it was because she heard a rumor that Brody was staying after school for a polo meeting. But still, you never knew. She was nervous just to meet Brody Carmichael's mom.

She hoped if she rode her bike like a madman, she could drop off the folder and ride out without seeing him. So Mina did just that. It was a fifteen-minute bike ride to Sunset Drive, and she was winded by the time she rode up to the palatial estate. Every house, including Brody's, was surrounded by tall walls and heavy iron gates. She pedaled over to the call box and hit the green button.

"No solicitors," a voice rattled through the high-tech electronic speaker. Mina looked around in surprise and saw that a camera next to the gate had zeroed in on her.

Mina pushed the green button once more and leaned in. "Um, I'm dropping off an information packet for Happy Maids. We were told to bring it by this afternoon." The voice didn't come back on right away. Mina assumed it was because whoever was working the voice box was checking with the Carmichaels.

"Name?"

"Mina Grime."

"Enter. Stay on the path. Don't ride that *thing* on the grass!"

The giant iron gates swung inward, and Mina rode up the driveway, mesmerized by the extravagance that money provided. What she had originally thought was the main house turned out to be the garage, which housed the family's vehicles. Mina's whole family plus the Wongs could all live comfortably in the Carmichaels' garage.

The main house sat back from the street, three stories tall with a terra-cotta roof. Majestic statues of horses were scattered throughout the estate, and Mina could see gardeners trimming hedges and mowing the manicured grass. Behind the estate were training yards and stables for the Carmichaels' horses. Their prized racehorses were probably at another facility.

This was the first time Mina felt acutely aware of her family's small income in comparison to others. She didn't really care about money, but she understood the phrase "out of her league."

She was embarrassed when she got to the steps of the main house and couldn't decide where to leave her bike. With the kickstand broken, Mina tried to lean it against a pillar and got a heated look from a maid. She went to lean it against a bush and received a horrified stare from the gardener. Giving up, Mina let it lie in the driveway, its back wheel spinning pathetically.

She took the front steps two a time and found herself in front of huge mahogany double doors with a silver mustang knocker. Knocking, Mina decided she would count to ten Mississippis, and if no one answered she would do leave the packet and go home. She'd only gotten to seven when Mrs. Carmichael herself opened the door.

Mina recognized the soft eyes and elegant smile, not to mention signature pearls and perfect coif, from the tabloid magazines.

"Yes?" Mrs. Carmichael asked sweetly.

"Hi, I'm Mina. I'm supposed to deliver this Happy Maids packet on behalf of my mom." Mina thrust the packet toward Mrs. Carmichael, hoping to get this delivery over with. Mrs. Carmichael wasn't cooperating, because she didn't take the packet.

"I'm sorry, what?" Her brow furrowed in confusion.

"My mother's boss, Terry Goodmother of Happy Maids, said you requested an informational packet. I'm just dropping it off for them." Mrs. Carmichael still looked confused, and Mina had a sinking feeling that this was a huge mistake. "I'm sorry. I must have the wrong residence." She turned away in embarrassment.

"Wait! What was your name again?" Mrs. Carmichael called out. Her eyes softened with compassion. Or it could have been pity.

Mina had made it to the bottom steps and turned to look back up at Mrs. Carmichael. "I'm Mina Grime."

"Mina. You're the one who saved Brody!" Her confusion disappeared and her face lit with happiness. "We have much to thank you for…oh, Brody, watch out!" she practically shouted.

Just when Mina had begun to wonder about Mrs. Carmichael's strange re-enactment, she heard a sickening crunch of metal on metal and turned to see her bike crushed to smithereens beneath the wheels of a black car. "My bike!" Mina groaned.

"Brody!" Mrs. Carmichael yelled simultaneously.

Mina froze. She didn't know what was worse—facing her long-time crush with a brown chocolate milk stain on her jacket, or the fact that he had just run over her pathetic bike with his expensive sports car.

The driver's door opened, and Brody jumped out of the car. "Mina, I'm sorry! Are you okay?"

Brody started to run up to them but then seemed to hesitate, stopping about halfway.

Mortified that Brody had run over her bike and with no good explanation as to why she was at his house, Mina could only think of one thing to do. Run.

It was obviously a terrible mistake that had sent her to the Carmichaels' house, and a cruel twist of fate that led to Brody driving up and crushing her red bike. Maybe if he had driven up and hit her car, it wouldn't have seemed so pathetic, but all Mina could think about was how when he asked his mother why she was there, it would seem like she was stalking him. It wasn't until she'd reached the main gates and run through them that she realized she had dropped the info packet on the ground. *Oh, no!* He would know that her mom cleaned houses for a living.

Mina heard someone call her name, but she ignored it and turned the corner. While she ran, tears formed in her eyes, and the cold wind swept them away. She wanted to die of embarrassment. Everyone at school would hear about how Mina made up some excuse to stalk Brody at his own house. How she made up a fake pamphlet so she could talk to him. How she was so desperate and poor that she rode her broken bicycle up to the mansion and how it was crushed like tin foil beneath Brody's expensive car.

If Mina were a stronger person, she would have confronted him about the bike, but when her whole reason for being there seemed fabricated, she lost her resolve.

It took Mina fifteen minutes to ride to the Carmichaels' house on her bike from school, but an hour to walk home from the Carmichaels'. She was tired, sore, and grateful that the rain had stopped shortly after sixth period. She couldn't imagine making this walk home in the rain.

When she finally reached the restaurant, Mrs. Wong called out to her. "Woo-hoo! Meenha. I seen you in pahper today. You beeg celebrity." She walked out holding a newspaper with a picture of Mina splattered across the front page.

The article must have been written before the assembly, since they used Mina's high school yearbook picture. Mina grabbed the paper and stared in shock. It was the worst photo of Mina in school history. She remembered that horrible day all too well. Mina had attempted to wear makeup, even put her hair in rollers so it would look like Savannah White's, and tried to wear something nicer than her signature hoodie. In the end, Sara got a flat tire, so Mina had to ride her bike in the rain. Mina's makeup, curls, and clothes were drenched for the photo shoot.

"Oh, no!" Mina grabbed the paper and crumpled it up. "Has my mom seen this?"

"Yes." Mrs. Wong smiled proudly. "I show her as soon as she got home. See!" She pointed to the front window of her restaurant, where she had made a collage of Mina's face as part of a giant display. "I advertise we have big star, live above us. Good for business. I bought every pahper from the store for miles." Sure enough, there were five stacks of newspapers piled neatly against the red and gold door. "Everyone that comes tonight gets complimentary free sample and pahper. Business is dooming."

Mina groaned and handed the paper back to Mrs. Wong. "You mean booming?"

"That's what I say, dooming." Mrs. Wong smiled, her eyes disappearing behind her cheeks.

Mina trudged up the stairs and unlocked the door to their flat. The neat and tidy apartment looked as if a storm had blown through. "Mom!" Mina called out.

47

Sara tore out of her bedroom with armloads of clothes and a wild look in her eye. She dumped them into an open suitcase on their kitchen table, and turned and pointed at Mina. "YOU! Go pack!"

"Mom, why? What's going on?"

"Don't you 'Mom' me." Sara looked panicked. "Do as I say, we're leaving." She flipped the lid on the suitcase and zipped it. Mina grabbed the suitcase from her mother, and they tugged on it until Mina won.

"No, I'm not packing unless you tell me why. This is crazy."

"Mina, we have to. It's for your own good."

Mina noticed her mother's eyes were rimmed in red, but if she didn't get answers now, she never would. "That might have worked on me when I was younger, but not anymore. Charlie will listen to you without arguing, but I won't. What's good for me is to stay here. I have friends. Well, a friend." For a split second Mina almost decided that moving across country wouldn't be such a bad idea, after the terrible last two days. But another look at her frantic mother gave Mina the determination she needed to make it through whatever disaster would unfold.

"You're still my daughter, and you will listen to your mother." Sara turned on Mina and put her hands on her hips.

"Yes, Mother, I will listen to you gladly, and do whatever you tell me to, AFTER you explain why we are moving." Mina was an obedient daughter, but she was also old enough now to shoulder some of the burden that plagued her mother. "Tell me why we keep running. I can help. Don't you think I need to know?"

Sara's expression didn't change, but her shoulders dropped toward the floor as if they carried the weight of the world, or at least one teenager. "I told you, it's for your own good."

"Is this because of the newspaper article? About what happened on the field trip?"

Sara didn't say anything. Her silence was the only answer Mina needed.

"It's because I saved someone's life isn't it?" Mina challenged. It was starting to make sense; a click went on in her brain that connected the pieces together. "You always discouraged me from trying out for sports, and clubs. You encourage me to not stand out and try to fit in, to not get noticed, to be a loser. You always feared something terrible would happen to me, but that wasn't all of it, was it?"

Charlie walked into the kitchen with a small blue leather suitcase and began inserting his most prized possessions: bubblegum, baseball cards, his rock collection. From a distance, there didn't look to be a single item of actual clothing. Ignoring the discussion between his mother and sister, Charlie wandered around the kitchen and began to pack up his cereals.

"But I finally accomplish something. I do something great like *save a life*, and for one day I'm a hero. Granted, I hate being the center of attention, but that's it, isn't it? You were afraid of something like this."

Sara sighed and collapsed onto a kitchen chair. She rubbed her small hands over her face in anxiety. "Something like that. I was trying to keep you from getting too much attention."

Mina stood motionless, confused and angry. "That doesn't make sense. Isn't that the opposite of what mothers are supposed to say? Don't you want me to succeed?"

"Darling, our family was meant for greatness, but the sacrifice that comes with it is too great. I thought if I could keep you away from the spotlight, if I could keep you hidden, then maybe we could outrun it."

"Mom, I don't understand." Mina began to shiver as a cold breeze wafted through the room.

Sara looked at her a long time before responding. "You're right. You're old enough to know the truth, to share the burden." Sara waited until Charlie had left the kitchen and headed for a second round of favorite objects to pack away. "Mina, I've lied to you about your name, about everything."

"Okay," Mina said, her voice sounding shaky.

"Our last name isn't Grime. It's Grimm. And for as long as I could remember, we've been trying to outrun it."

"Outrun what exactly?"

"Outrun what killed your father years ago...the Grimm curse."

CHAPTER 5

She felt as if her world was spinning uncontrollably. "I think I need to sit down," Mina said pathetically. Sara jumped from her chair to grab her daughter and led her to the small uncomfortable couch in the living room.

Mina was about to ask more questions, but Sara held up her hand to stop her. "Please, sweetie, let me explain." Taking a deep breath, Sara tried to gather her thoughts before proceeding. "It goes farther back, to your great-great-great-grandfather, Wilhelm Grimm, and his brother, Jacob."

"The Grimms. Do you mean the ones who wrote the fairy tales?"

"Yes, the very same. And no, they didn't write most of them. They collected them. But more importantly, they actually lived the tales. It's part of the curse that plagues the Grimm family. Each generation is cursed, chosen, fated to relive the tales. It is why the stories keep changing throughout history, as each Grimm's action or decision changes the outcome."

"Do you mean like Cinderella doesn't always get the prince?" she joked.

"This is serious, but yes. More often than not, the stepsisters do."

"Oh, come on, Mom. You really believe this stuff? This is what is making you pick up and run? Why not try to get the prince and live in the castle?"

"Because that's not how it works." Sara looked frustrated; she kept gnawing on her bottom lip as she pondered her words carefully. "You don't get a choice in the tale. You don't get a choice in the part you play, and if you remember, they don't all have happy endings. Do you think everyone could survive reliving these tales? Your Uncle Jack didn't."

Mina's jaw dropped in shock. "But I thought that was an accident?"

Sara shook her head. "The curse followed your uncle, and then when he died, it latched onto your father. Strange things started happening, but he ignored the warning signs. He believed that he was smarter and stronger than his brother and could make it through the stories till the end."

"Is there a way to stop it, to break the Grimm curse?"

"It's believed that if a descendant of a Grimm can survive all of the tales, then the Story will be satisfied. Your father survived ten tales before he died." Sara started crying and buried her face in the couch's throw pillow.

Mina felt her mouth go dry, and she had to lick her lips and clear her throat before she could ask the next question. "How many tales are there total?"

Sara looked up, sniffed, and then looked over at her daughter. "Oh, sweetie, I won't let it find you—it's why I changed our last name and why we keep moving. Every time we move, it seems to take longer for the tale to find us, even longer if we don't do anything special to get ourselves noticed."

"How many?" Mina repeated, feeling the strange tingling sensation throughout her body.

"We don't have to stay. We can keep running, and it won't drag you into the tale. You won't suffer the same fate as your father."

Mina stared at her mother hard.

Sara finally broke eye contact and whispered out, "Over two hundred. Jacob and Wilhelm together made it through over one hundred and ninety, but they couldn't complete all of them before they died. So then it started over again with Wilhelm's children. Honey, they were the only ones to even come close to breaking the Grimm curse, and that was almost two hundred years ago. More Grimms have tried to overcome it but didn't survive, like your father. So I decided to try to run from it instead."

"Mom, I don't want to run."

"Mina, we have to. I didn't think the curse would pass to you because you were a girl. Your father assured me that the curse only passed to the males. After he died, I thought we were safe. I didn't know I was pregnant with Charlie until a few weeks after the funeral. Once I knew it was a boy, there was really no choice. We had to run and leave behind our past, even your father's name, to protect his future.

"I knew one day it would eventually come for Charlie, but I never expected it to choose you. It wasn't until I saw you in the backyard talking to a frog that I realized your father was wrong. Too many of the fairy tales had a female heroine, and you were too gifted and kind-hearted for the story to ignore."

"You make it sound as if it's alive."

"It is. There is something far greater at work here than what the human mind can process. It's ancient, it's old, and it's powerful. Some say it's God, others say it's fate, but whatever it is, it can't be stopped."

"What about Charlie?" Mina asked. Her brother was back in the kitchen, and this time he was putting on every single piece of costume he owned, layer after layer. A Spiderman suit,

Batman's utility belt, and what looked to even be a Doctor Who scarf and hat.

"So far the story isn't interested in Charlie, not when it has you."

"So as long as I live, Charlie is protected?" Mina looked over at her brother and felt her heart grow with a single-minded determination to protect him.

"Yes…honey, look at Charlie. He's not strong enough to protect himself from the fate of the Grimm Story. I can't lose you, and I can't lose Charlie. You two are all I have left of your father." Sara grabbed a few tissues from the box on the beat-up coffee table. She picked at them, tearing them apart.

"Mom, I want to try to stop it." Mina didn't know where her courage came from, but as soon as she said it, she knew it was true.

"No! I forbid you. Nothing strange has happened since the field trip, right? We still have time to run." Sara looked at Mina, and she could see the sliver of hope in her mother's eyes.

"Mom," Mina said, packing as much meaning into that one word as she could.

"It's too late, isn't it? What happened? What's been happening?"

Mina mentioned practically riding over a dog and donkey, and was shocked when Sara blurted out "and a cat and rooster" before Mina had even finished. Sara blushed. "I've read up on my tales. Anything else? Tell me exactly what happened on the tour," Sara demanded, and Mina did. "Oh, this sounds bad. It sounds like it could be another story, but I don't know which one. It may already be too late. Well, at least that stupid book hasn't appeared yet."

"What book? Grimm's Fairy Tales?"

"Mina, trust me, it's better if we don't discuss this anymore. Words have power, and it makes it that much easier for the Story to find you."

"What about the book?" Mina asked again.

"Again, it's better to not to mention it. The book is called The Grimoire. It's the final piece of the puzzle. Once it's found you, you know it's too late. You are officially part of the Story's tales. Only problem is, other things are looking for the book as well. So it's best we leave before either of them find us." Sara stood up and looked around the small living room, furnished with only a sofa, television, and a small rocker. A rarely used fifteen-inch TV was in the corner, nestled against a few tattered books given to them by Mrs. Wong. There were hardly any personal items in the home, and Mina finally understood why.

"Mom, I'm not leaving," she said.

"Yes, you are. Think of your brother." Sara blinked at her daughter in disbelief.

"I am thinking of Charlie, and that's why I'm not leaving." Mina could feel herself begin to cry again, and pushed back at her tears with the back of her sleeve. "I'm going to stop this. I can do this. I will do this, for him, for you."

Sara started to shake her head, but Mina continued angrily, "Mom, you can either help me or hinder me, but one way or another, the Story is going to catch up to us."

Sara sat down again and looked at her hands folded in her lap. Tears slowly slid down her cheeks to land in wet drops on her khaki pants. "I don't know if you can fight it. I wish we could postpone this until you are older, stronger."

"I'm both, Mom. You did great, but now it's my turn to take care of the family. But I'm going to need your help."

Sara wiped at her own tears, and nodded her head in understanding. "Okay. What do you need me to do?"

CHAPTER 6

Walking to school the next morning, Mina felt like a completely different person. She had answers to questions that had been plaguing her for years, though not all of them. She knew why her family moved so much, why her mother always discouraged her from trying out for sports, from submitting to her school paper, or trying to get noticed in any way. She felt as if her crazy teenage life now had meaning, a purpose. She was a Grimm, and had a legacy to uphold. The fate of future generations of Grimms depended on her to finish the Story and break the curse on her family.

Mina had plenty of time to think over everything as she walked to school. She had told her mother about the mix-up at the Carmichaels' and the fate of her bike, but had convinced her not to call up the Carmichaels in a fit and to let it go.

"Really, Mom, it was my fault, not theirs. I left the bike in the middle of the driveway. Plus, I wouldn't have been there if your boss Terry hadn't gotten the families mixed up."

"I don't understand—there's only one Carmichael family. And you said they weren't expecting us? Pretty strange."

Mina darted out of the door the minute her mother picked up the phone to call her boss. As it soon started to sprinkle, she wished she would have checked the forecast.

A tingling sensation on the back of Mina's neck alerted her that she was being followed. Picking up her pace, Mina kept her head up and tried not to make eye contact. She was preparing to bolt when a car pulled up next to her and rolled down its window.

Mina wasn't sure what to expect: robbers, kidnappers, perhaps someone who was going to ask for directions and then force her in their car. What she didn't expect was the polite way in which the driver asked, "Need a ride?"

"No, thanks," Mina shot back. She picked up her pace, refusing to look at the driver. The rain started to come down in bigger droplets, making her squint.

"Mina...please."

Mina's head turned in surprise to see Brody Carmichael driving alongside her in his SUV. She faltered in her footsteps but kept moving. How did he find her? How did he know where she lived? She knew her phone number and address were unlisted.

"Mina, I'm so very sorry about your bike. It was an accident." Brody looked apologetic. Mina kept walking. "The least you could do is let me give you a ride to school. It's raining."

It was raining, hard.

Mina blinked the rain out of her eyes and shivered. Whether it was from the cold or the idea of sitting less than a foot from Brody Carmichael, she wasn't sure. But when her teeth started to chatter, Brody darted out into the rain and ran to the passenger's door to open it for her. "Get in, before you get sick."

Mina bobbed her head in answer and slid in, her wet jeans sticking miserably to the leather. Her hair was now soaking wet, and large drops of water were dripping onto the seats of his car.

"I'm sorry." Mina's teeth chattered as Brody ducked back into the car.

His large hand went to the console and turned on the heat. He twisted in his seat and reached behind him to pull a clean shirt out of his gym bag. "Here, use this." He took the shirt and gently tried to wipe the water from her face.

Mina jumped from the touch, and he held out the shirt in a peace offering. "Sorry," she said again.

Brody smiled out of the corner of his mouth. "You sure do apologize a lot, when it's not even your fault."

"I'm getting your seat all wet." She tried to use the shirt to wipe off the pools of water on the leather, but he reached out and touched her hand, stopping her efforts.

"It's just a car. It'll dry." He looked at Mina, and her heart fluttered. He meant it; he wasn't lying or trying to appease her. He didn't care about the car at all.

Mina let the heat of the car soak into her bones—no, wait, those were Brody's heated seats. She was so nervous; she didn't know what to say or where to look. Should she talk to him, look at him, ask him about his family? She couldn't decide, so Mina did none of these things, staring quietly out the passenger window instead.

Brody cleared his throat. "You know, you're one hard person to find."

Mina turned to look at him. "What do you mean? You were looking for me?"

Brody cast her a quick glance before focusing on driving again. "Well, I tried to call you to apologize, but you were unlisted, and then no one I knew had your cell number."

"I don't have a cell phone." Mina felt her cheeks turn pink; she must be the only girl in high school without a phone. "I'm also not friends with anyone you would know."

Brody shrugged. "I didn't know. So then I was going to come to your house, but again…"

"Unlisted," Mina finished for him, glad for once that her mother paid a small fee to keep it that way. She didn't know what she would have done had Brody showed up on her doorstep in the middle of yesterday's tearful confession.

"Brody, it's okay. What happened yesterday was an accident. I left it in the middle of the driveway. It wasn't as if you ran me over." Mina played with the edge of her sleeve. She was doing it again, taking the blame.

"Then why did you run from me?" Brody asked, looking at her. "You didn't give me a chance to apologize or explain."

Mina hadn't anticipated this question and now desperately wished she was back outside, walking in the rain. She lifted her shoulders pathetically in reply. "I don't know." A few minutes of silence filled the car, and then Mina turned on Brody. "What were you doing on this side of town this morning? I know for a fact that you live on the other side of town."

Brody chuckled and smiled at Mina. "Looking for you."

"For me? Why?" Mina was numb with disbelief.

"I felt bad about what happened and wanted to find you. So I had one of our employees do some digging, and found out you lived in the international district. So I decided to head over here to find you. I mean, I did destroy your only mode of transportation. The least I could do was drive you to school."

"And lock me in the car so I have to listen to your apology, right?" Mina pursed her lips in anger. She couldn't believe him. He had someone do a background check on them? "You had no right!" she said.

"I had every right." Brody pulled the car into the school parking lot. He put the car in Park and turned toward her, the windshield wipers still moving back and forth in rhythm with the rain. "I knew that if I didn't find you outside of school, I might never get to apologize."

Mina scoffed. "Oh, I understand. I mean, after all, you're Brody Carmichael, and you have a certain social standing to uphold. I'm just Mina Grimm, a nobody." Mina realized she'd let her real name slip, but he didn't seem to notice. He opened his mouth to argue, but Mina cut him off. "It's okay. You've apologized, see? Apology accepted. You've done your civic duty, and now you're off the hook. Don't worry—we aren't going to sue or anything." Mina grabbed for the door handle and exited the car, fuming at his nerve.

Doing everything she could to keep from running into school, Mina marched as quickly as possible toward the girl's bathroom and locked herself in a lone bathroom stall. She couldn't believe she just had a fight with Brody. Tears burned in her eyes from embarrassment and anger. *How could he?* she fumed. Why would he go to all the trouble to search her out, to apologize, when he could have just done it at school? It's because she was right—he was embarrassed by her. Too bad that she, boring old Mina, had saved his life, and not some more exciting girl. If only he knew.

Mina wiped away her tears and walked to the sink to compose herself. The rain had added a slight wave to her brown hair, which was not unattractive. It fell past her shoulders and was mostly dry, thanks to the awesome heaters in Brody's car. She suddenly felt queasy as she remembered what she'd said to him in anger. She hoped that it would all blow over and he would forget her.

The first warning bell rang, and three girls rushed into the bathroom to apply a final layer of makeup before class.

"Did you see Brody out there?" one girl whispered. "He looks angry. I wonder what Savannah said to tick him off." She pulled a giant can of aerosol hairspray out of her backpack and began to spray it all over her head.

Mina started to cough and back up from the sink.

"Didn't you hear?" a brunette commented between mascara swipes. "They are officially over."

"Since when?" the chunky one asked.

"Since that day when he almost died."

"But I thought they got back together?" Aerosol Girl commented.

"Only for a few hours. I heard he broke it off after school."

"Excuse me," Mina interrupted, and all three heads snapped in her direction. Each of them appraised her, and the chunky one frowned in disapproval. "Did you say that Brody is outside these doors?"

"What's it to you? Thinking you're going to move in now that he's single? I can tell you right now, you're not his type." The dark-haired girl and the heavier girl laughed.

"Actually, I'm trying to avoid him."

The dark-haired girl appraised her once more before she answered, "Not anymore. He was pacing outside for a few minutes, but I saw him head toward his first class."

Mina sighed. "Thanks." She rushed out of the bathroom and made it to her first-hour class just in time for the second bell. Mina slid into her desk, and Nan immediately leaned over and whispered,

"Is it true?"

"Is what true?" Mina whispered back, pulling out her history textbook.

"That Brody drove you to school. Are you two an item?"

Mina couldn't believe how fast things spread in this school. "No! He gave me a ride, and that's it."

"But I saw…" Nan started.

"Please, Nan, I will tell you at lunch. I promise."

Nan must have seen the anguish in her best friend's eyes, because she let the subject drop. Sighing, she leaned back and looked at her brand-new iPhone, a gift from a friend of the family's after they learned she dropped it trying to help Mina and Brody. Nan's fingers gently tapped a response to the text message she received moments ago.

Upset. Give time.

CHAPTER 7

"Spill," Nan demanded once they had taken their trays far away from prying ears. Mina had selected the table farthest from the one Brody sat at with his friends.

"It's entirely your fault, Nan. I went to deliver the stupid packet because you wouldn't do it. And after totally embarrassing myself in front of Mrs. Carmichael, who had no clue why I was there, Brody drove up and ran over my bike."

"O-M-G!" Nan spelled aloud. "What did you do?"

"I was so embarrassed, I ran."

"You WHAT?" Nan jumped back and slapped the table.

"Exactly. And when I got home, my mom had gone on a packing binge and was ready to move us to Alaska."

"But how does that lead to this morning?"

"He stalked me! He got an employee to find out where I lived and then drove up and down my streets like a stalker. Supposedly he wanted to give me a ride because he felt bad for crushing my bike."

"Um, Mina," Nan said softly.

Mina ignored her, peeling her orange with a vengeance. "Yeah, and then he had the gall to tell me he wanted to apologize before we got to school, because he knew he wouldn't once we were *in* school. Geez, he is SO stuck up."

"Mina—" Nan tried to interrupt her friend as she attacked her helpless fruit.

"I'm telling you, Nan, he is afraid to be seen in public with me. Even after I saved his life and all." Mina shoved an orange slice into her mouth and bit down.

"Mina, I think someone wants to talk to you." Nan smirked.

"MFFWHA?" Mina said, her mouth stuffed with orange. She looked around the cafeteria and saw that Brody's usual spot with the polo team was empty. He was, in fact, standing behind her, tray in hand, looking perhaps more embarrassed than she was.

"Hi, Mina." He smiled. "Is this seat taken?"

Brody dropped his tray on the table without waiting for her to answer. How much had he heard? Once she had stopped coughing, she turned on him. "What are you doing?" she whispered, looking around the room. People were staring at them.

"I know you thought our conversation was over, but it's not," Brody said, his blue eyes twinkling with challenge.

"All right, you've proven your point. You're not embarrassed to be seen with me in public. So you can go now." Mina made shooing motions with her hands as if shooing away a fly, but Brody just grinned at her.

"You see, what you said in the car made me angry. Until I realized that it's not true." Brody leaned over to get closer to Mina's ear. "I'm not embarrassed to be seen with you in public. You are. You don't want to be seen with me." His breath tickled her ear, making her melt until she'd processed the words he spoke.

"That's not true," she replied.

"Then prove it," he said. His eyes darkened with meaning. "Prove to me you're not ashamed of me."

Mina looked at Brody fearfully and then over at Nan, who had wisely kept her mouth shut. Nan nodded encouragingly at her. Mina hung her head in shame. It wasn't Brody she was embarrassed about, it was herself. She was a walking, talking embarrassment, and why in the world would Brody want to hang out with her?

"Why, Brody? Why do this?" Mina asked, looking up at him. "I don't understand. We have nothing in common. I've saved your life, but that's as far as this friendship needs to go…really."

Brody looked hurt. Mina wished she could take back the words as soon as they left her mouth, but she was only trying to protect herself. He had to be playing with her.

Brody stared at his tray of food for a minute and then looked up at her. His eyes bored into hers. "Mina, you did more than save my life, and I'm trying to show you. But you have to meet me halfway." He picked up his tray and walked away from their table, dumping the uneaten contents in the trash. Students turned to watch him walk out, and they kept turning until they were looking toward Mina's table.

One student in particular couldn't tear her eyes away from Mina. Her eyes flared angrily when Mina caught them on the way up from her phone's screen, and she did not look away. Mina looked at Nan with wide eyes, hoping she'd just imagined what she'd seen: Savannah White, the most popular girl in school, mouthing the words "you're dead."

***

The rest of the day dragged on. Mina never got to speak with Nan about the Grimm family curse, and nothing interesting appeared or followed her around school, so Mina hoped the Story had forgotten about her. Mina was so preoccupied with the Grimm curse, Savannah, and Brody that she was pretty sure she flunked her history test. She felt numb as she handed an almost blank test to her teacher.

When the final 3:30 bell rang, Mina breathed in relief. She could now go to the public library and try to research more about her family's history. Walking to her locker, Mina was surprised to see the number of students surrounding it. She decided to hang back and wait until the crowd dissipated so she could grab the rest of her books and leave, but the number didn't budge. Putting her head down to enter the mob, Mina clumsily maneuvered to her locker, stepping on toes, saying, "excuse me," bumping elbows. It wasn't until someone grabbed her elbow to steady her that she saw the reason for the crowd of students. Brody was leaning against her locker, and he was holding her elbow.

"See you guys later!" Brody ordered the crowd. Unbelievably, the group of students left until it was just the two of them.

"How do you get used to it?" Mina asked.

"I've dealt with it all my life, so I learn to tune it out." Brody looked sad until he turned to Mina and his face lit up with delight. "You ready?" he asked.

"For what?" Mina looked around, confused.

"To go home."

"Of course," she answered, reaching behind him to open her locker. She grabbed her backpack, embarrassed by its pathetic state. Dropping it in her hand, she tried to move away from him, but he snatched the backpack and hoisted it on his shoulder.

"Hey, give that back! I can carry my own backpack," she said, putting her hands on her hips.

"I know, but this way I guarantee that you will follow me."

"Don't count on it," Mina grumbled, stopping in the hallway, refusing to budge. When she saw that Brody just kept walking, even turning the corner with her backpack still in hand, she had no choice but to follow meekly behind.

Once she caught up, Brody turned around and started walking backward. "See, I know you."

"No, you don't. You just met me," Mina countered.

"But I would like to get to know you," Brody said, smiling. "If you would let me."

Brody walked them out to his car, and once again he opened the door for her. Once Mina was safely inside with her seatbelt buckled, Brody started the car.

"Where to?"

"I thought you knew everything about me. So you should know where I live."

"Uh, not really. My father's friend had problems pinpointing the exact address. He only knew the area. Why is that?" he asked. "Are you hiding from the mob or something?"

"Or something," she answered. "Can you take me to the library?"

"The library! My, aren't we studious." Mina rolled her eyes and went for the door, but Brody stopped her again. "Hey, I'm kidding around. The library it is." He turned the key in the ignition and pulled out of the parking lot, putting on their local pop music station for their drive. The silence seemed to draw a wedge between them, but Mina wasn't going to be the first one to speak. A few exits later, they pulled into the parking lot of the town's small white library.

Mina jumped out as soon as the car pulled to a stop. "Thanks for the ride. And sorry. You know, about earlier. I'm sure you're a nice person." She gave Brody a fake smile, and grabbed her backpack and shut the car door. Brody's door opened, and he shut his door after her. "You don't have to stay," she told him. "I'm going to be here for a while."

"I'll wait for you. You're even farther away from home than before, and I'm definitely not letting you walk home alone."

"I can call for a ride. My mom will be home soon," Mina said, speaking quickly. This was definitely not a research trip she wanted to share.

Brody looked at her. "Mina, you are not getting rid of me that easily. I'm already here. Let me help you."

"I don't need help."

"All right. Then let me come and do my own thing. I need to study, too, you know." Brody swung his own bag over his shoulder and walked up the steps through the glass doors. Once again, Mina had no choice but to follow behind.

Mina loved the smell of libraries, loved the smell of old books and the soft hum of the lights. It was probably why she was so out of tune with kids her age. She didn't watch a lot of TV, and she spent more time reading than socializing, except for hanging out with Nan.

Once she'd shooed away Brody, Mina walked past Mrs. Toole, the head librarian, stopping only long enough to wave, and headed straight for the reference section. Scanning the numbers and stopping at 398.2, Mina began pulling out various collections of tales and individual stories.

"What's with the fairy tales?" she heard suddenly, and again there was Brody, taking the books from Mina to stack them against his chest.

"Homework," Mina replied distractedly. "I thought you had some of your own."

"What classes are you taking that you get to read kids' books?" he said, reading the spines. "Maybe I should take it."

Mina grinned. "It's for a project at home, not school. And I can carry them myself." She grabbed the stack from Brody and made her way to an empty table in the back of the library.

Sitting down, Mina grabbed a book and began searching for clues while keeping a corner of eye alert for Brody and his habit of sneaking up on her. Within a few minutes she saw him stretching out at a table nearby, reading a small paperback. Mina found it difficult to do any reliable searching with Brody sitting a few feet from her, and he didn't look uncomfortable at all. She would have thought that he would be antsy and dying to get out of the library.

She found herself unable to stop sneaking glances, enthralled with his lanky posture, the way his blond hair fell over his eyes as he turned the pages. He seemed content, at peace. Once, his eyes met hers and she blushed in embarrassment, hoping he didn't think she'd been staring at him. After two hours of trying to concentrate, reading as many fairy tale histories as she could, she slammed the latest book closed, feeling fatigued. Brody had barely moved, but looked up at her with a worried expression.

"Come on, let's get you something to eat." He took the book from her hand and laid it on the table.

"No, I'm fine...really." Mina's heart started to beat faster with worry. If she went to get food with Brody, that would be too close to a real date.

"I'm hungry. I didn't eat much at lunch today." Heat rose up the back of her neck as she recalled that he'd dumped his lunch in the garbage. This time, she didn't argue.

They left the library, and Brody drove toward a small '60s drive-in, where he ordered hamburgers and fries for them both at the speaker box.

"I didn't know they still had these," she said in awe.

"Yup. Isn't it great? My parents took me here all the time when I was a kid. I was obsessed with the speaker box, so my parents always let me order for everyone. One time I ordered eight milkshakes, so we drove them back and gave them to our staff." Brody smirked, his eyes twinkling with mischief.

Mina was stunned by his good looks and completely lost her train of thought. When the food came, they ate and talked about funny stories from their childhood. At one point, she realized Brody was watching her out of the corner of his eye, and secretly smiling.

"What's wrong? Do I have food on my face?" Mina asked, suddenly nervous.

Brody threw his head back and laughed. "No, but why do you ask?"

"You've got a funny look. What's wrong? You can tell me."

"I'm smiling because I can't figure you out. You're different. You don't act like other girls."

"Oh...I see." She remarked unhappily and put her French fry back into its container. She had lost her appetite.

"No, you don't see." He turned in the seat so he could face her. "Look at me." Mina kept her head down. "Mina, please look at me." He very gently reached over and with one finger lifted her chin up so that her brown eyes bored into his dark blue. "You are unlike any girl I've met. You don't talk incessantly about hair and makeup. You tell me what you're feeling, instead of telling me what you think I want to hear. You're content to sit with me without filling the silence with needless chatter. You eat food, real food, not rabbit food." He plucked up the fry Mina had put back in her container and ate it in one big bite. "And you're not constantly texting or talking on a cell phone."

"I don't own one," Mina reminded him.

"Exactly, and I like that about you."

"You like that I don't own a cell phone? You must be crazy."

"Maybe I am," he said with a small smile. "Just being with you has a calming effect on me, do you know that? My life is so…hectic. So many people surrounding me, trying to be my friend, trying to tell me who I should be and what I should become, that I tend to tune out the real world. I spent so long going through the motions just to make the background noise fade, but when I'm near you, it's gone. The pressure to be something or someone I'm not is gone."

"Oh, well," she started, stunned and unsure what to say. "You're welcome, I guess. More fries?" Brody laughed, and took her up on her offer. They ate the rest of the meal in comfortable silence, sneaking smiles at each other. Mina had never felt happier. Brody had now spent a few hours in her presence and still seemed to be enjoying her company. She wasn't sure what this would mean when they got back to school, but for now, it was bliss.

Mina asked to be dropped off a few blocks from home. "If my mom sees you, she will flip. She's not too happy that you destroyed my bike."

Brody became still. "I understand," he said quietly, too quietly. He pulled over and watched Mina get out of his car.

"Thanks," she called to him through the open window and waved. As soon as he was out of sight, she ran home to call Nan.

***

The next morning followed a similar routine. Brody appeared on Mina's street and picked her up as she was walking to school. To Mina's great surprise, he sat with her at lunch as well.

She was actually starting to like having Brody as a friend, if she could quit thinking about what revenge Savannah might have planned. So far it was only nasty rumors that Nan, queen of all social media, quickly dismissed. Of course Nan was thrilled to have Brody at their table and talked nonstop the whole lunch hour. Brody would shoot Mina smirks when Nan would go on a rant about one of her reality shows. He seemed to enjoy her company as well.

Mina looked for Brody by her locker after school, and felt a pang of sadness when he wasn't there. Maybe he had gotten tired of her? After all, she wasn't that exciting. Mina opened her locker to grab her bag, and when she shut the locker, he was right behind the door.

"Oh! You scared me." Mina put her hand to her heart.

"I would never do that on purpose."

"If I didn't know better," Mina frowned at Brody, "I'd say you're definitely stalking me."

"Of course. I'm trying to prove to you that I don't care about social status, and you promised to give me a chance." Brody grabbed her backpack and marched off with it toward his car.

"I promised no such thing," she said after him.

When she caught up, Brody reached for her hand, and they walked to his car hand in hand. Mina felt as if she was on cloud nine, but a shiver of doubt cast a shadow on her happiness. This couldn't be happening. It just wasn't right, just didn't fit with the long string of bad luck that had followed her all her life. Brody high-fived one of his friends on the way to the car, a jock who'd never be caught dead speaking to her. Nor did she belong with someone like Brody. She was used to the stares and whispers about being an oddball, but ever since Brody started paying attention to her, the whispers had gotten worse. She even got a rude letter shoved into her locker after lunch, probably from one of Savannah's friends.

She stopped ten feet from Brody's car, refusing to take another step.

"Brody, really, this is unnecessary. It's a little overboard, with the rides to school and back, sitting with me at the lunch table. I think you've proven your point. You were right—I was the one who was uncomfortable with you, not the other way around. And I think you've paid back your debt." Mina stood as still as she could, half-hoping and half-dreading that he would confess.

Brody refused to let go of her hand. With his other hand, he lifted her petite chin so she could look into his eyes. Were people looking? Mina tried not to care. "Please believe me when I say that this isn't about a debt I owe or a bet to prove myself."

"I feel like this is some sort of sick joke, and you're trying to mess with my emotions." Mina turned away from his touch.

"This isn't, believe me." Brody leaned forward, tantalizingly close to her mouth, but a bunch of catcalls and whistles alerted them to their very loud teenage audience. Mina stiffened when she overheard someone call her a *Grimey Gold-digger* and quickly pulled away, but not far enough that Brody couldn't steer her back toward his car. She got in it without a word, happy to be out of sight. For the rest of the ride she stared out the window in silence, ignoring Brody's worried glances, lost in her thoughts.

Grimey Gold-digger? They thought she was after Brody for his money? It was the farthest thing from the truth. Yes, she had secretly crushed on him from afar, but it had nothing to do with his money. This was worse than she had imagined. Mina was so distracted by her own inner monologue that she was surprised when Brody pulled up to the library again.

"How did you know?" Mina asked, speaking for the first time since entering the car.

"I knew that you were looking for something pretty hard yesterday, and it didn't look like you found it. Maybe if you tell me, I can help you look for it today?"

Mina shook her head. "I don't know what exactly I'm looking for. All I know is that I'll know it when I see it."

Brody followed Mina into the library with his book bag, and they headed toward the table she'd sat at before. This time he brought homework and was content to sit with Mina as she pored through encyclopedias, journals, and microfiche film. After another three unsuccessful hours, Mina was ready to give up.

"You didn't find what you were looking for, did you?" he asked.

"Afraid not." Mina leaned back in her chair and rubbed her eyes. "I'm going to check another shelf. I'll be right back."

Brody raised one eyebrow at her in disbelief.

"I promise I won't run off without telling you. After all, I don't want to walk home."

Mina walked a few aisles down and peeked through the shelves to spy on Brody. What was he doing here? She couldn't fathom why he would want to hang out with her, especially in a library. She would have thought he would have gotten bored and gone home already, but to stick with her for two whole days? Leaning against the shelf, Mina felt defeated.

She was here to look for a clue, not pine over Brody. She needed a sign, anything to help her family.

Yesterday she had finally convinced her mother to tell her everything she knew about the Grimm family curse and the Story. Supposedly there were signs that would appear to tell her she was the chosen one. Like the appearance of animals. Sara also explained that once she was chosen, the Grimoire would appear, a book of power that was supposed to aid her.

"How do I get the book?" Mina had asked, feeling as if she was already losing precious time in breaking the curse.

"You don't," Sara told her. "It will come to you."

"What do you mean? Didn't Father have it, and Uncle Jack before him?"

"Your father did, but after his passing the book disappeared. Its own way of protecting itself, I guess. When the Story chooses the next Grimm member, the book decides if it's going to help them."

"What do you mean, it decides?" she'd asked. "Shouldn't it just automatically help the next family member?"

"Unfortunately, no. The book goes into hiding, and then it chooses whether or not to appear and help. What if the next Grimm descendent wasn't honest, was greedy and selfish? What if they were evil? The Grimoire would be a terrible weapon in the wrong hands. So it must protect itself, and after you've been weighed and tested, then it will make itself known to you."

"That sucks." Mina furrowed her brows in thought. "Where did it appear to Dad?" she asked.

"In a library in Nebraska."

"Okay. So what about our library?"

"Worth a try," Sara said, shrugging,

Mina sat in silence as she thought through her options. "Why is it called a Grimoire, anyway? I thought that was something evil, or a book of spells or something."

"No, honey, it's just a record of the tales your family members have lived through. Over time it has gained powers of its own. If your ancestor's name was Smith, it would have been called the Smithoire. But, Mina, are you sure you want to do this? We're talking about very powerful magic." Sara then spent the next hour trying to talk Mina out of following through on finding the Grimoire.

In the library, her first approach was to open up every book on fairy tales and see if she could find the Grimoire. It looked different according to each person who held it, her mother had told her. So it could be disguised as a children's book, a magazine, a Bible, anything.

But maybe it wouldn't appear to Mina, because she hadn't yet proven herself worthy. Apparently saving Brody Carmichael's life wasn't enough. Mina was about to give up when something white caught her eye, and she stood up. Bending down, she tried to see between the shelves and over the books. There it was again, a flash of white. Following it, Mina crept along, keeping herself low to the ground. There! She caught a glimpse of white feathers. What? The feathers surprised her, and she stopped in her tracks, confused. Was this some kind of joke?

After a moment, Mina hurried to catch up to her prey. The way it moved made her realize this wasn't human but definitely a bird. The animal made a squawk, confirming her suspicions, and Mina followed the noise down a corridor. Maybe it was a clue and would lead her to the Grimoire. She ducked into another aisle and saw that she'd been chasing a goose, which was now headed toward a back emergency exit.

The door was already propped open, and she watched as the bird stepped through it.

Running after the goose, Mina plowed through the emergency exit door and came into a dark back alley. The sun had set, and steam rose from the sewer grates behind the library. Almost instantly the hair rose on Mina's arms in fear. Something was wrong. Turning, she tried to catch the door back into the library, but it had shut and locked automatically.

Mina strained to get her eyes to focus, but there wasn't any sign or a single stray feather from the stupid white goose. It had disappeared. Another tingling feeling began in Mina's body, and she recognized it as a warning sign. She was reacting to the power of the Story. Something or someone was here.

CHAPTER 8

A low growl made Mina turn with her back to the door. A large man stepped out of a darkened doorway across the alley and came to stand before Mina. He looked primeval, with long black greasy hair, a pointed nose, and golden eyes that seemed to reflect the light. His chest was bare, covered only by a worn black vest.

"Give it to me and I'll let you live." The man's voice rumbled deep in his chest, more animal growl than human.

"Give you what?" Mina asked, stepping back in fear.

"The Grimoire." The man stepped closer but still kept his distance, keeping one foot out of the protective circle cast by the light.

"I don't know what you're talking about," she said, proud that her voice didn't crack with fear.

"Stupid girl. We know the Story has chosen you. Where is it?" he growled again, his lips pulling back from sharp-looking teeth.

"I d-don't have it," Mina stuttered. "It hasn't shown itself to me. I swear." The man flexed his fingers and walked into the circle of light, illuminating a wolf tattoo that covered his whole chest. Mina yelped and backed farther away until she felt the hard door behind her back.

"Then you must die." The man with the wolf tattoo lunged at Mina and grabbed her upper arms. Mina tried to run under his arm, but he was too fast, inhumanly fast, and within half a second he had her around the waist. Screaming for help, she kicked and punched, vainly trying to make contact. The man turned her swiftly and hit her hard in the face, then lifted her as if she was a rag doll and tossed her off into the alley. Mina's scream was cut short as she landed in a pile of cardboard boxes, better than concrete but still hard enough to knock the wind out of her. Her face throbbed in pain.

The wolf man sauntered toward Mina, who was nearly paralyzed with fear, and grabbed the front of her blue hoodie in one fist. With a grin that showed off his sharp teeth, he lifted Mina into the air, her Converse dangling helplessly below her. She felt tears come as his grasp on her collar began to choke her, and she began to see spots. She dug her nails into the man's hands, hoping to loosen his hold, but he only seemed more excited at the sight of the blood. Darkness began to fill her vision, along with grief for her mother and brother. She had failed them before her quest had even gotten started. She had nearly resigned herself to her fate when she saw movement out of the corner of her eye.

A loud crack split the air, followed by a howl of pain. Mina was dropped to the ground and went limp, struggling to regain her breath. Opening her eyes, she saw Brody standing over her attacker with a broken 2x4. She tried to tell him to run but couldn't catch her breath; her throat was on fire. The man was stunned for a minute and then lunged at Brody, clumsily grabbing his midsection and knocking him to the ground. Brody held his own and fought back, landing a punch in her attacker's lower jaw. The man must have been dazed, for after a few unsuccessful lunges and missed punches, he finally ran off, swearing at her.

"We will be back, and one way or another, we'll get it," the man howled.

Brody was immediately at Mina's side. "Mina, are you hurt? Are you okay?" He ran his hands gently up and down Mina's arms, searching for broken bones, but his touch sent shivers up them instead.

"I'm fine," Mina answered, trying to shake off Brody's warm touch.

Brody grabbed Mina's face between his hands and searched her face for bruising. She let the tears come freely now, grateful to have a kind-hearted person by her side, to have survived the attack, to be alive.

Brody helped Mina to her feet and then tucked her against his side protectively. She leaned into Brody's chest for support and took comfort in his arm wrapped around her shoulder. Breathing in the warm scent of his shirt, cologne, and sweat, Mina felt safe, secure, until she stumbled on her own feet.

He must have felt Mina falter, so, without waiting for her approval, he bent down and picked her up in his arms, intent to get her out of the alley and somewhere safe. She protested, but not for long. When he got to his car, he put her inside and buckled her in. Mina knocked his hands out of the way, trying to get him to quit messing with her seatbelt, to let him know she wasn't helpless. He smiled and handed her the buckle.

He peeled onto the road and pushed on the gas, making the high-performance car accelerate with barely a sound. It wasn't until Mina saw that he was going forty over the speed limit that she thought to panic.

"Brody, slow down!" she yelled.

He pounded the steering wheel in frustration, his blue eyes stormy with anger.

"STOP! If you're going to drive like a crazy person, you'll have to let me out!" When Brody didn't seem to hear her, she began to panic, grabbing the door handle for safety.

Finally he got his temper under control and slowed the car down. "I'm so sorry, Mina. I should have been there to protect you." He reached out to touch her bruised cheek, but Mina flinched back in fear. He dropped his hand dejectedly. She had hurt him unintentionally.

"You see, now you're scared of me. I'm not angry at you—I'm angry at myself that you got hurt." Brody looked at Mina, and she could see fear written in his eyes.

"Brody, it could have been worse. A lot worse. But you saved me." Mina gently reached out to touch Brody's arm, to comfort him, to show him that she wasn't afraid.

"Who was he, Mina?" Brody's jaw clenched and unclenched in anger.

"I don't know," Mina answered truthfully. "Some guy in an alley. An evil, evil man."

She watched as Brody's knuckles turned white on the steering wheel. "He threatened you, and you don't know who he was. He seemed to want something. He said he'd be back."

"I told you, I don't know who he is. And I don't have what he wants." Mina felt her own anger rise.

"But you know what it is?" Brody asked, unbelieving. "If you know what he's after, then give it to him."

"I don't have it, and even if I did, I couldn't give it to him. You have to believe me."

"Maybe I could, Mina, if you told me what's going on?"

He looked at her accusingly, but Mina's silence was the only answer that Brody got.

"Please take me home now," she said a few minutes later.

"Absolutely not! We need to go to the police."

"No, I want you to take me home. I don't want to go to the police, and if you take me I will deny everything." Mina turned on Brody angrily. "I never asked you to get involved, I never asked you to sit with me and chauffeur me around. Hanging out with me for two days does not give you permission to decide what I should and should not do. Besides, this would never have happened if you hadn't run over my bike! I never asked for your help, and I don't want it. Take me HOME." The last words flew from her mouth, and she instantly regretted her tone. But it was too late to take them back; the damage was done.

Neither of them spoke a word until they reached the international district, delineated by faded Mexican stands and restaurants, and the occasional Chinese joint. She demanded he stop one block from her home. "Stop, here!" She pointed, and Brody pulled over.

"Mina, I'm sorry!" Brody began but was interrupted by Mina's sudden exit from the car.

Mina quickly slipped between the colorful stalls and people, trying to lose him. She waited until his car pulled away into the night and she could no longer see his taillights. When Mina was sure Brody wasn't on her street, she ran all the way home, trying hard not to look over her shoulder. She grabbed her key to the blue street-level door, ran straight up the stairs, and yelled goodnight to her mom, claiming she was tired. Once safe, Mina crawled into bed, cradling her hands around her knees, and cried herself to sleep, wishing she hadn't stumbled on the Pandora's box that was her family's curse, and wondering how she'd ever survive.

CHAPTER 9

Mina had the full intention of going to school the day after the attack by covering her bruises with makeup. She was about to tell her mother about the attack at the library, but then decided against it when Sara took one wide-eyed look at the bruise and began to shake. Mina quickly played it off as another clumsy gym class incident, which was not uncommon for Mina, and it seemed to ease her mother's fears.

If Sara found out that her daughter had been attacked by a large man in the alley, she would make them run again, Mina knew. She went to the small closet that housed the family's laundry and reached into the dryer to pull out a clean hoodie. "What the...?" Mina said aloud. The hoodie she'd pulled out was red, and she hated the color red.

She reached up to pull out another zippered jacket. This one was red, too. In fact, all of Mina's hoodies were now permanently red. Her mother had warned her that the Story would try to mold Mina's lifestyle into a fairy tale, but she didn't believe it until now. When she went to show her mother, she could tell it shook her, perhaps more than anything that had happened so far. Sara didn't blink an eye when Mina asked to stay home from school. Something about the red jackets terrified her mother into compliance.

Sara went on a one-woman war against the color red. She threw every piece of red clothing in the house in the garbage. She scoured the house high and low for every red ribbon, washcloth, marker, and pen, and even burned the red Christmas stockings. Gone. All of it, gone.

Sara bought Mina new clothes and a few new hoodies at the local Target, despite their limited budget. She brought home blue, lavender, and white zippered jackets to replace Mina's other ones.

They lasted a day. The next morning, Mina opened up her closet to find another sea of red.

She pulled down a hoodie that she knew yesterday had been a beautiful royal blue; it even said so on the tag. Today it was a deep red. Mina grabbed the next jacket, and the next. All red. Thankfully, none of the denim had been changed, so she grabbed a pair of jeans and matched them with a red shirt and red jacket. Otherwise, she'd have looked like a bright red tomato.

These events only encouraged Mina more. By Saturday, she was even more determined to find the Grimoire. She had to, as she knew her very life, and that of her brother, depended on it.

Hearing voices, Mina entered the kitchen and smiled when she saw Nan Taylor sitting at the breakfast table with Charlie. Nan wore a stocking cap over her blonde braids and had layered two long- and short-sleeve shirts. She had already helped herself to a bowl out of the cupboard and filled it with three different cereals. Charlie had a huge grin on his face exactly parallel to Nan's deep frown as she dug in.

After she managed a few bites without puking, she stood up and pointed her finger at him. "Ha! I'm telling you, I have a stomach of steel. I can eat any kind of concoction you come up with." Nan did a little victory dance around the table, and Charlie shook his head and pointed to his own bowl of cereal.

Frowning, Nan leaned over to look at his bowl. "What? I used the same cereals that you did! I've got Cocoa Puffs, Lucky Charms, Raisin Bran, and Mini Wheats. What else could you have fit in there?" There was obviously some contest going on between the two, and Charlie was finding a discrepancy in the winner.

Nan was one of the few people who had no problem carrying on a one-sided conversation with Charlie. Considering that she usually talked enough for three people, anticipating what Charlie was going to say was probably easy for her. Or so Mina guessed.

Nan picked up Charlie's spoon and began to dig around in his bowl to see what else he'd put in there. "I don't see it. I made mine the same, and I ate half of the bowl, so I win, pipsqueak." Dropping the spoon into the bowl with a clank, Nan leaned back and put her foot on the table. "Pay up."

Charlie grinned again and shook his head no. Standing up, he went over to the small refrigerator and yanked the door open. A few seconds later he emerged holding a brown bottle of caramel syrup. Walking over, he put it down next to Nan's half-eaten cereal bowl with a satisfied grin. Nan sat up in disbelief.

"NO WAY!" She leaned back over and looked closely at the tan-colored milk in Charlie's bowl. Her victorious grin faded as she realized what she had to do. "That is some serious sugar going on there. How in the world do you sleep at night?" Nan asked respectfully. She never criticized Charlie, or ridiculed him for his weird eating habits, but praised him for his uniqueness. "So I have to add this to my cereal, huh?"

Charlie's smile got wider.

Nan gulped visibly, and her hand wavered for an instant in front of the bottle, but she took one look at the smiling boy and regained her resolve. Popping open the top, she poured a few good tablespoons into the bowl and mixed it up with her spoon, watching Charlie the whole time. Right before her first bite, she paused and pursed her lips in thought. Suddenly she jumped up and went to the fridge, rummaging around inside, and came back with a white and blue container. Retrieving a clean spoon, Nan scooped a huge tablespoon of the mixture into her cereal. Charlie's face went green with disgust. Charlie hated cottage cheese, and Nan knew it.

Fearlessly, Nan stared down the eight-year-old boy, grabbed her spoon, and dipped it into her intensely gross breakfast. She put a huge spoonful into her mouth and chewed slowly, even thoughtfully, as if she were tasting all the flavors. Charlie watched Nan chew in awe before he visibly paled and started to gag. The boy dropped his spoon and raced for the bathroom.

As soon as the bathroom door slammed, Nan turned to the sink and spit out the mouthful of food. She turned on the water and leaned forward to rinse out her mouth. When that didn't work, she reached back into the fridge and grabbed a container of orange juice and began to chug right from the container.

"Nan, that's disgusting." Mina laughed.

"Tell me about it. I'm the one who actually had to taste the thing. I don't think I'll be able to eat cottage cheese again." She gargled orange juice.

"What possessed you to put cottage cheese in the cereal?"

"When I saw what Charlie was eating, I challenged him to a contest. Winner gets to pick out a movie and make the loser watch it. Believe me, I had no idea he added caramel to his cereal. Blech!" Nan shuddered dramatically.

Mina had forgotten that Nan hated caramel almost as much as Charlie hated cottage cheese. "So you thought you would cover the taste of caramel with something else you liked?"

Nan bobbed her head. "Yeah, I actually love cottage cheese and thought it was a great idea, and would surely make your brother freak out and I would win. The only problem was that when I added the cheese to the cereal and put it in my mouth, it took every ounce of strength not to immediately eject it out. My mind thought the milk had gone bad. But I did it–I won." Nan began to do a victory dance around the kitchen.

Sara walked in and looked at the bowl in front of Nan, turning her nose up. "Okay, Charlie has taken it too far, he's wasting cereal. I paid good money for those boxes."

Nan looked sheepish and grabbed the bowl away from Sara. "No, Mrs. Grime, that's actually my cereal. I'm having breakfast with Charlie."

Sara raised one eyebrow at Nan.

Feeling pressured to prove her point, Nan took the spoon and shoveled another gross spoonful into her mouth, screwing her face into a big fake grin.

Satisfied, Sara busied herself in the kitchen while the girls hid their laughter. "Where is Charlie, anyway?"

"Bathroom," Mina answered quickly. When Sara went back to her bedroom to grab her keys and wallet, Nan spat the cereal out into the garbage and began the sink and orange juice routine all over again.

Mina took the bowl of cereal away and dumped it down the garbage disposal, removing any hint of Nan's stupidity. "So now that you've won, what are you going to make Charlie watch?"

"I don't know, I was thinking of something really horrible like the whole first season of Power Puff Girls, something completely girly and embarrassing." Nan's face lit up with the prospect of torturing Charlie. "Or maybe I could find a documentary on the making of cottage cheese."

"You do realize that you would have to sit through it as well."

"Hmmm, then that won't do. What do you suggest?"

"Why don't you pick something you'll both like?"

"What?" she squealed. "That takes away the whole fun of the competition! NO! He must suffer." Nan pointed her finger in the air dramatically.

Mina thought Nan would have made a great sibling if her parents hadn't divorced when she was young. Neither one remarried, making Nan the quintessential only child: loved, spoiled, and a little lonely, which was why she enjoyed hanging out with Charlie. Nan always said if she had a younger sibling she would want a brother, because then she wouldn't have to share her clothes.

"Don't you mean YOU must suffer?" Mina conjectured.

"Meh, whatever." After Nan had finished with her tirade, she directed her radar Mina's way. "So dish."

"About what?" Mina asked casually.

"About WHAT? I can't believe you. I didn't drive all this way for nothing on a Saturday morning. I have cartoons to watch. Dish about what happened two days ago that made you miss school and send Brody into a coma."

"He's in a coma?" Mina panicked.

"No, not literally. Yeesh. He's been walking around the school like some sort of zombie, not talking, just completely withdrawn. Something happen between you two?"

"You promise it's not going to show up on any web page, interview, tweet, or text?" Mina knew when dishing important info to Nan that she had to cover all her bases.

Nan rolled her eyes and held up two fingers. "Boy Scouts' honor."

"You're a girl."

"Fine then, Girl Scouts' honor." Nan held up three fingers.

"Don't think it counts if you've never actually been a Girl Scout," Mina countered, making sure there were no loopholes in her friend's credibility.

Mina looked over Nan's shoulder toward her brother and mother's room and decided that they needed to find a more private spot. Tapping Nan's shoulder, she motioned down the hall and into her room. When the door was securely shut, Nan jumped across Mina's hastily made bed. Mina perched on the end more daintily.

"Nan, I'm cursed."

"Yeah, I know. We all are." Nan kicked her legs back and forth and grabbed a magazine from Mina's nightstand. "It's called being a teenager. You, more so, because you live in the Stone Age."

"No, my last name isn't even Grime, it's Grimm. What I am telling you is, I am personally cursed, or fated, to follow the same path as the Grimms before me." Mina already felt better now that she'd gotten it in the open. She had been thinking for the last few days on how to break the news to her best friend.

Nan just stared at Mina, blinking her eyes in thought. "Yeah, right. I'm supposed to go to Yale and become a lawyer like my father and his father before him, but do you see me treading down that path? No way, Jose. I'm hitchhiking to

Julliard instead." Nan flipped a couple more pages and then oohed over a cute skirt.

Mina snatched the magazine from Nan and sat on it so her friend couldn't grab it back. "I'm serious, Nan. I'm in over my head, and I need your help."

Nan sat up and gave Mina her full attention. "You're really serious?"

Mina ran her hands over her head. "Dead serious."

"Like, this isn't some trick to try to punk me or anything, right?"

"No. I wish it were, I really do, but it's not."

"Okay, I'm listening. Start from the beginning." Nan crossed her legs Indian-style and waited patiently through Mina's whole tale. She barely fidgeted, never once interrupted, and even didn't immediately grab her phone to tweet the update. "Whoa," was all she said when Mina was done.

"You can say that again," Mina mumbled unhappily.

"Whoa," Nan repeated, and ducked as Mina threw a pillow at her. "So you were actually attacked outside the library? That must have been awesome."

"Nan!" Mina chided. "NO! I could have been killed."

"But you weren't—Brody saved you. So if Brody saved your life and all, then why is he in such a fit?"

"I'm not sure, but I probably have something to do with it. He wanted me to go to the police, but if I did, and my mother found out, that would be the end of us. She would have shipped us out to Canada before you can say…'Canucks.'"

"So you two fought," Nan stated.

"Yes, we argued, and I demanded he drop me off. And with a huge bruise on the side of my cheek, I couldn't very well go to school." Mina paced her small bedroom and kept passing her bedroom mirror to look at the bruise.

"So in other words, he hasn't called you, spoken to you, or seen you since the attack." Nan ticked off the words on her hands. "That definitely explains why he has been out of sorts. MINA, CALL HIM! Let him know that you are still alive."

"Nan, I can't." And Mina truly felt that she couldn't. She had burned her bridges, and burned them badly.

"Nonsense, all you do is pick up the phone and say, 'Brody, I'm not dead.'" Nan grabbed her phone and held it up to Mina's ear. "Here, you can use my phone."

Mina glared at Nan in response.

"Fine." Nan put her phone away. "Since it seems you have a lot to do, maybe we should get cracking and find this Grimoire or whatever and prepare you to break the curse." The way Nan said it made it sound as if Mina was going on a camping trip and needed to find supplies, instead of possibly meeting her doom. "But before we do anything else today, we need to eat!"

"You just ate," Mina said.

Nan made a gagging face. "That is not what I would call eating. That's biting the bullet to win a bet. I'm starved. Let's grab food first. You owe me."

After a cheap lunch at one of the Mexican stalls nearby, the girls walked the rows of small shops in the various districts.

"So your dad...?" Nan let her question trail off. It was too delicate a question to ask outright.

"Yeah, my dad was chosen by the curse before me and was caught in one of the more vicious tales. He didn't live through it." Mina walked a little slower.

"Do you remember the night?"

"No. I guess I must have suppressed a lot of those memories, and my mom won't speak about it. What I do remember was that my dad was happy, loving, and carefree until my uncle died. That's when it all changed. He changed. He was driven, obsessed with breaking the curse."

"He must have loved you a lot."

"That, or he wanted revenge for Uncle Jack. I don't know." Mina felt at a loss, confused, and a little angry. "So I HAVE to do this, Nan. I have to finish the tale and break the curse, because if I don't, it falls on Charlie, and I can't let that happen. I have to protect Charlie."

"Sign me up—where do we start?" Nan said.

"Nan, you don't have to help. You don't even have to get involved. I only told you because I needed your support in case I have more episodes where I can't go to school."

"You can't tell me about this curse and then NOT expect me to help. I'm your friend. I care about you, and I care about Charlie. It's a done deal."

"Nan?"

"Don't you 'Nan' me—I've got two semesters of karate under my belt, a serious case of attitude, and mace on my keychain. I'm ready to tackle any giants that come my way. Fe Fi Fo FUM!" When she said "Fum," Nan did a karate kick in the air and followed with a chest punch.

"I think that's the wrong story." Mina laughed.

"What, there's no giants? I was really hoping to tackle some giants." Nan looked devastated.

"From what my mom said, the tales don't necessarily fit the Grimm guidelines to a 'T.' They adapt to the modern world. Yes there are giants, but it maybe instead of a thirty-foot giant, you may find yourself facing a six-foot-six, 300-pound New York Giant football player."

"I'll take that!" Nan gushed excitedly. "Bring 'em on." When she had quit jumping around on the sidewalk, doing martial arts moves and knocking into complete strangers, she stood up suddenly and looked at Mina.

"Yeah, for some reason the Story is the driving force behind all of this. We can never underestimate and never trust the Story."

"So what happened on the tour was a fairy tale story? So cool, which one?" Nan was walking backward and kept throwing quick glances over her shoulder.

"I have an idea, but it doesn't make sense." Mina put her fingers in her jacket pockets. Shaking her head, Mina decided it was nothing and kept walking.

"So how do we go about finding this book? You said your father found it in the library. What about your uncle? How did the Grimoire come to your uncle?"

Mina face turned down in anger. "It never came to Uncle Jack."

"But I thought you said that it comes to the Grimm descendants and helps them?"

"I did, but it doesn't always decide to help them. It chose not to reveal itself to my Uncle Jack. It didn't help him, and now he's dead."

"But, Mina, it came to your father, and he still died." Nan put her hand on Mina's shoulder and looked into her face. "All we can do is pray that it chooses to help you."

Mina nodded her head and took a deep breath. "I'm just so scared. Nan, what if it doesn't choose to help me and I'm stuck trying to fight off more people like the man with the wolf tattoo alone. I can't do it. I need its help, and I'm scared it won't help me." Mina sniffled, trying to hold back the tears.

Nan grabbed her friend in a huge hug. "Mina, you're the sweetest, most kind-hearted person I know. The Grimoire will come to you—how can it not? And if it doesn't, you've got me, and I'm ten times, no, twenty times more helpful than a book. I told you not to wear that hideous dress to homecoming, and you didn't. I kept you away from that disastrous-looking egg salad at the buffet, and then everyone else got sick. I even stood up for you when someone made fun of you for always wearing hoodies."

"Someone made fun of me?" Mina asked. This was the first that she had heard about that.

"What matters is that I'm here for you, and with me on your side, you will always win." Nan grinned and put her arm through Mina's.

Her best friend was right. With Nan's gumption and determination, they could face anything. There were times when Mina felt as if she was kryptonite to anyone who came near her, except for Nan. Nan was immune to Mina's bad luck and seemed to thrive off warding it away. It was almost as if Nan was her personal good luck charm.

"Oohh! We have to go in here and see the puppies!" Nan squealed and forcefully dragged Mina into Pawpers Pet's. The door jingled when they walked in, and immediately Mina was hit by the scent of dog, urine, and bleach, so strong it nearly knocked her over. She fought the urge to breathe through the sleeve of her red jacket, knowing it would give Nan a reason to tease her.

Mina didn't care for pet stores. She loved animals, but hated going in and seeing hundreds of caged dogs, cats, birds, and mice. To her it was the same as walking into a prison and being asked to pick out a cute inmate to take home and care for. She sighed and walked over to Nan, who was already gushing over a playful Pomeranian and American Eskimo puppy.

"Oh, aren't you the cutest? Yes, you are! You're the sweetest thing since cotton candy," Nan was saying. The pups yipped and crawled over each other in an attempt to lick the glass window where her hand rested. Before long, a cute red-haired employee spotted Nan's interest and offered to bring the puppies to the viewing pen. Nan squealed with glee. "Did you hear that, Mina? We can hold them and play with them." By the time Nan turned back, she was nearly as excited as the puppies in the kennel. Somehow Mina didn't want to be stuck in a 4x4 cubicle with the hyperactive Nan and two pups.

"Uh, I think I'll pass this time. I'm going to check out the rest of the pets." Mina backed away from Nan, who was already adrift in her own world. She got an indifferent look from Greg, who was busy either sizing up his new customer or trying to score Nan's number.

Leaving the two of them, Mina walked past the parakeets and canaries, when a melodic whistle made her stop and turn in surprise. The canaries were singing. She leaned in toward the birds slowly to listen to their song, careful to not startle or interrupt them. They fluttered about their white cage, seemingly impervious to Mina's nearness. When the singing stopped, Mina froze, hoping that they would continue their song, but she noticed that the canaries weren't the only birds to stop singing. All of them stopped making any kind of noise at all. The macaws, parrots, doves, and parakeets were silent, and stood unmoving in their cages. Never in her life had Mina walked into a pet store and heard this kind of silence.

She swallowed nervously and began to back away from the bird aisle and make her way back toward Nan. The canaries turned their heads and watched her retreat. Being under the scrutiny of so many black beady eyes was enough to make anyone jumpy. "It's just a coincidence," Mina chanted to herself. "It's just a coincidence." Mina was so nervous that she stumbled into a large fake tree stand with a gray macaw. The bird crooked his head and snapped his beak a few times before it spoke one word. "Doom."

CHAPTER 10

The hair stood up on the back of Mina's neck. "Doom, doom, doom," the parakeets echoed. The silence disappeared as all of the birds seemed to chirp one word over and over: "Doom. Doom. Doom." Even the canaries seemed to take up the banter.

Mina covered her ears and ran down the aisle, putting as much distance as she could between the bewitched birds and herself. She didn't stop running until she was in the aquatics department.

"Finally!" Mina muttered. The sound of the birds dissipated into nothingness among the hums of the stacked fish tanks. Looking around at the fish tanks, Mina was relieved. There was nothing here that could talk and spew out frightening words. The fish, either because they had small brains or were numb to humans, ignored her presence next to their tanks.

Mina walked aimlessly, staring at the different fish and thinking back to what had just happened. Had she imagined the birds speaking to her? Or was this more of the Story's magic trying to take control? There wasn't any way the canaries could talk, so maybe she had imagined it.

A thumping noise drew Mina's attention toward a shelf of tanks along a side wall. There wasn't a tag identifying the species in the tank, but the presence of logs and moss gave her the idea it was some kind of amphibian. *Thump, thump.* The noise came again, and Mina leaned closer to look to see what was making the noise. Something smacked itself against the glass, causing Mina to scream and step back. She could clearly see it was a toad, who was not only croaking but throwing himself against the glass as if trying to break through.

Thump! Thump! More thumping sounds came from one tank over. Mina stared in horror as frog after frog came out of hiding and began to throw itself against the tanks. Eight tanks full of frogs in various sizes began to shake and move with the vibration of the frenzied frogs. Even the tree frogs were causing their smaller tank to shudder the slightest bit.

"Stop it!" Mina hissed out. "You will hurt yourself." She reached forward apprehensively to push the tank with the large toads farther back on the shelf. The toads took this as a rally point and began to climb on each other's backs as a way to reach the top of the cage and lift the lid off.

Mina looked around in horror and grabbed a large aquarium rock to weigh down the lid. The other amphibians must have gotten the same idea, and began to hop, climb, and otherwise maneuver to the top of the tank so they could escape through the lid.

"No, no, no, no," Mina called out frantically, and looked for other decorations to keep the frogs from escaping. She put a pink mermaid statue on the tree frogs' tank, and petrified wood on the poison dart frogs', which could have been disastrous. It wasn't until something slithered past her foot that Mina abandoned her efforts. A large striped snake was disappearing under a shelf, and, from the looks of it, more snakes were dropping from them by the second. When a boa came toward Mina's legs, she screamed and ran toward the front door. She only hoped the frogs were smart enough to stay in their tanks once the snakes were loose, but that wasn't her problem anymore.

Mina slowed by the puppies long enough to grab Nan's arm by the elbow as she was handing one of the puppies back to Greg.

"Nan, we have to go. Now!" Mina whispered under her breath. A little louder, she called out toward Greg, "I think there's a clean-up in aisle eight."

Greg looked up in surprise and went to get a doggy bag and broom. Mina knew Greg was assuming he needed to clean up whatever present a customer's unattended dog might have left for him. Unfortunately, it wasn't going to be that kind of surprise. She secretly hoped Greg wasn't afraid of snakes.

Once they were back on the sidewalk, Mina kept up a fast pace, causing Nan to nearly run behind her. "Mina? What's the matter? What's going on?"

Mina didn't answer until they were three blocks away, and by then she was out of breath. "Birds," Mina huffed. "Doom. Frogs, snacks, I mean, snakes. The frogs and snakes—they came after me!" Mina tried to make sense, but her lack of breath and her own disbelief made it hard for her describe. How could she explain to Nan what she hardly believed herself?

"Well, in other news, that creepo gave me his number," Nan commented dryly, while staring back in the direction of the pet store. "The glasses were cute, but he is totally not my type."

Mina was taken aback at the calm way Nan spoke, how unaware she was of what had almost happened in the store. Nan shook her head and looked at Mina. "What were you saying again?"

Her mouth dropped open, and then she stuttered, "U-uh forget about it." Nan grinned and grabbed Mina's arm.

They walked arm in arm until Mina had settled down. She let Nan's mindless chatter calm her nerves until she could focus on the matter at hand. "Please," Mina prayed quietly to herself, "I need to find the Grimoire. I can't do this alone."

The search for the Grimoire was beginning to seem hopeless, and after the scare in the pet store and alley, she knew she probably wouldn't live through one Grimm fairy tale. She had just about given up when she felt the tingling start, which usually accompanied magic of some sort. She felt all her limbs stiffen, but there was no clear and present danger in their path. Mina carefully looked up and down the block. Everything appeared normal, just a busy commercial street with regular people going about their day. The story wouldn't do something so public, would it? She slowed her walk but only felt the tingling intensify.

Turning to warn Nan, she tripped over a welcome mat and kicked at it angrily. Then she noticed the animals woven into the mat's design. It looked very old. She glanced up at the building in fear. There wasn't a marquee or name on the building front, just a precariously hung wooden sign printed with the same picture, that of a bull and stag.

Was this the Grimoire, or another of the Story's games? She had come too far not to find out. Mina pulled on Nan's arm tentatively and led her into the building, which was unlocked.

The quiet tinkle of a bell announced their entrance in a small dark store.

"Hello! Anyone here?" Mina called out when no one came to greet them.

"Maybe they aren't open yet?"

"Nan, the door was unlocked."

"Maybe the owner stepped out. I'll step outside to see if there's a number posted."

Mina started to stop her but realized it was probably for the best. If something dangerous was down here, she didn't want Nan to get hurt. "Why don't you go next door to Rosie's Flowers and see if they know who works here?" she suggested.

As Nan stepped out, Mina had the distinct feeling that someone, or something, was watching her. Turning around in a circle, she took in the dark oak shelves, the paisley wallpaper, the dimmed and burned-out lights. A check-out table and old cash register stood off to one side and looked as if they hadn't been used in ages. The place was dust-free but had the feeling of being empty for a long time, or at least empty of anything living.

A large chair stood to one corner, and Mina had begun to walk toward it when she heard the distant sound of children laughing.

"Hello? Who's there?" She took a few hesitant steps in the direction she'd heard the noise. "You can come out—I'm looking for a book. Maybe you can help me?"

A glow began in the back of the store, and the sounds of children laughing intensified. Mina gulped, but followed the light as it grew brighter and seemed to pulse with its own rhythm against a back wall. When she finally reached the wall, the light disappeared, and she was encased in darkness. Letting her eyes adjust, Mina turned and was confronted with a pair of red angry eyes. Jumping back, she stumbled and knocked into something furry that shifted from her weight. Mina screamed.

When nothing reached or lunged for her, she reached out her hands to touch the angry glass eyes she had seen earlier. They were part of a life-size giant bull, but it was either fake or dead. She wasn't sure she wanted to know. Behind her stood another life-size animal, this one a very large stag, frozen on his hind legs.

The stag and bull were lifelike and magical in their realism, neither touching the ceiling nor the floor. They'd been set about six feet apart in front of an intricately painted forest mural. The stag was on his hind legs, head angled as if challenging the bull. Mina touched the soft fur of the stag and felt heat emanating from the life-size pieces. The stag swayed and slid a few inches to the right. Pressing her head to the wall, she could see that the animals were attached to sliders on the wall. Perhaps it was some sort of puzzle.

Taking a few steps back, she looked at the two animals and decided that they were on the verge of being joined in battle. The bull looked angry, but the stag bore another expression entirely; it seemed fearful and determined at the same time. This must have been a very talented taxidermist. She first went over to the heavy black bull and pushed as hard as she could, half expecting it to come alive at any second. Grunting and biting her lip, Mina struggled with the bull piece until she had moved it to the center of the wall.

When she knew she had pushed it as much as she could, Mina tackled moving the large stag piece. Unbelievably, it slid with ease toward the bull, almost eagerly. But at the current rate, as she pushed the stag, she realized it would be positioned dangerously in front of the bull's horns. The thought made her uncomfortable, so when the stag had nearly reached the bull in battle in the exact center of the mural, she pushed up so the rearing stag would have the advantage. She turned and heard an audible click over her shoulder, followed by ominous creaking.

Mina only had a moment to react as the giant bull unhinged from the wall and fell forward toward her, horns aiming for her heart. Leaping to the left, she dodged the heavy piece as it collided with the stone floor under the stag, breaking in half. When the dust settled, a door appeared where the bull was moments before. "How can that be?" Mina thought. There was nothing there but the mural moments ago.

Dusting off her hands, she looked toward the stag and blinked in surprise. It was gone, but there was no door where the stag had once been. She supposed she had no choice but to try the door that appeared behind the defeated bull. She opened it slowly, looking behind her shoulder for Nan, reminding herself that it was better if she weren't involved. The door led to a dead-end circular room built of large stone blocks. She looked around the walls for clues but found nothing but solid stone. Wait!

Below her, there was something carved into the floor. Crawling on her hands and knees, Mina did the best she could to wipe away what looked to be hundreds of years of accumulated dust. Whoever cleaned the shop upstairs hadn't bothered with this place. Her fingers could feel the distinct outline of something. Getting excited, she blew on the engraving, scattering dust particles everywhere. They were all over her clothes and hair, making her sneeze, but that didn't deter her.

"So that's where you went!" Mina spoke quietly as her fingers traced the outline of a fighting stag, glorious antlers in full array. It looked as if it were a seal or cover for something. Mina stood up and looked around the room for something to break the seal. Finding nothing, she turned and stepped on the stone circle in an attempt to head out of the room, but the ground shifted beneath her, causing her to drop to her knees.

The stone circle was dropping from underneath her into what looked to be...nothingness. Scrambling, Mina leapt away from the circle and dug her fingers into the cracks between another stone in the floor. The stone circle stopped moving and waited almost patiently until her fingers gave out and she slid back into the hole to land ungracefully on her backside. Once properly seated again, the stone circle continued its descent, although slower, as if not to scare Mina further. It didn't help; she was still terrified. Finally she heard a loud thump, and the floor stopped moving. She could tell by a burst of air she'd descended to a larger room, though it took a few minutes for her eyes to adjust in the near-total darkness.

Mina wasn't sure how she'd get out of here, and thought about calling for help, but felt power gathering again, warning her that something was about to happen. Never leaving the circle of light cast into the hole, Mina waited. A small voice inside warned her to not step off the stone circle. What if it decided to float to the ceiling again, shutting her in the dark forever? What if she ran into the bull out there? There were too many "what ifs" to convince herself to not leave the stone tablet. That was, until her eyes alit on a clear glass coffin.

Mina averted her eyes, afraid of what she might see within. It could have been the bones of a small child or animal. When her mind was through playing tricks, Mina cast another glance to see that the glass coffin was not a coffin, but a glass chest. Instead of holding the remains of someone who had passed away, it held a yellowed scroll. Her heart began to thud with anticipation. Was this it? Was that the Grimoire?

Everything was surreal, misty and cloudy like a dream. Mina had no choice but to step off the stone and approach the chest to open it. Fortunately, it opened as soon as her fingers touched the lid. The scroll began to unwind of its own accord, and the yellowed paper seemed to resonate with a hum of power. Upon the scroll were words written in many different languages and dialects, along with beautifully crafted pictures.

As she stared in awe, the painted pictures began to move and walk and speak. She heard voices and singing, the same children's laughter she'd heard upstairs, all coming from within the scroll. Reaching a tentative hand up to touch the scroll, Mina recoiled as it shifted and fell heavily to the bottom of the coffin, now a large leather-bound book.

Wow, that's huge, Mina thought. *How am I supposed to carry that around?* She watched in amazement when the book, as if hearing her thoughts, slowly began to shrink into a smaller, thinner book. Mina felt like cheering. She had done it. She had found the Grimoire, and it was even shape-shifting to suit her needs. It would help her.

"Thank you," she whispered to the book. Then, after some thought, "That's still rather conspicuous," she said out loud. Another bright light appeared, and the small book morphed into a school math book.

Mina laughed out loud. "Better, but not quite. I'm terrible at math." Mina encouraged the book to keep trying, and it finally changed again, this time into a slim red spiral notebook.

"Perfect. No one will expect a notebook."

She picked up the notebook and was surprised by how light it felt. She was even more surprised to learn that it was blank. The pictures were gone, the writing—everything had completely disappeared.

"So how are you supposed to help me?" She held up the book to the light as if expecting an answer. Feeling slightly let down, she touched the cover lightly and whispered, "I hope you know what you're doing, because I sure don't." The book seemed to warm up in answer.

Mina took the notebook and tucked it under her arm while stepping back onto the stag platform, hoping and praying it would take her back up into the world above. She breathed a sigh of relief when the stone rose into the air, taking Mina with it. It thudded softly as it clicked back into place. Mina was now back on the first floor. But as soon as her feet left the seal, the color seemed to fade from the room. It was as if she had unplugged the store from its battery source, and it was now draining. Walking a little faster toward the front of the store, she tripped on a rug and saw that the store itself was shrinking! The shelves had gotten closer together, and the rugs were moving beneath her feet.

Mina began to run and had to dodge as slowly books, figurines, and various pottery on the shelves started to topple over. At first it was only a few items, and then she heard *thunks* and glass shattering all around her. The walls began to twist, and a few papers flew past her, knocking into Mina. She had to hurry and get out.

Running now, she saw the entrance, but by now the door she'd first entered was two feet smaller. Mina threw her shoulder into the red door, and it gave out with little resistance. She flung herself out of the room with both feet, landing in a heap on the sidewalk, scraping her elbows and knees on the hard cement. She never knew the Grimm curse would be so physically exhausting.

Groaning and brushing grit from her damaged elbows, she turned over to look at the store and saw…a blank brick wall. The building had disappeared! Sitting up, Mina looked to the left and saw the pottery store and Rosie's Flowers, but there was no longer an unmarked store in between them, just a plain brick wall. Quickly getting to her feet, Mina tried to not draw any more attention her way; she was already getting a few uncomfortable stares. Where was Nan?

Something felt wrong. The sun wasn't where it was supposed to be; it was almost evening. Mina looked at her watch and saw that it had stopped at 1:11 p.m. When she glanced at the clock in the square, it was closer to 7 p.m. Mina had been in the store for six hours? That wasn't possible, was it? Why hadn't Nan ever come back in? Where was she?

Instead of waiting, Mina decided to head home, cutting through the back alleys between roads, something she had done hundreds of times before, so she could call her friend. She never noticed when a dark shadow separated from the wall and followed her.

CHAPTER 11

As the man neared, Mina felt the dread run across her spine, giving her an instant in which to react. She jumped back, but the attacker made a grab for her hoodie. She heard the tear of cloth as a piece ripped off in his hands.

"Little girl, you should know better than to traverse dark alleys alone. Tch tch tch."

The familiar voice made Mina shudder in terror. How had he found her? It was the same man with the wolf tattoo who assaulted her behind the library. The man chuckled and sniffed the ripped piece of her jacket, and began to rub it along his face as if learning her scent. His hands looked longer than humanly possible, and his nails were dark and dirty.

"Leave me alone, or I'll scream," Mina threatened.

"Oooo. I like it when they scream," the wolf man countered, taking another step forward. Using his long fingernails, he tore the piece of cloth easily, like a knife through butter.

Mina bolted. Holding onto the notebook, she ran like crazy down the alley, desperately hoping to make it to the road before he caught her. But speed was on her attacker's side as she was jerked backward by the hood of her jacket, smacking her tailbone against the pavement.

Mina jerked away as the man made a grab for the notebook. She bit his hand and he roared. The notebook fell and was flung open. Mina tried to scream, but he lunged for her throat and began to squeeze.

"Please, somebody help me!" Mina choked out. The wolf man was about to backhand her when a blurry form leapt toward him and knocked him off her.

Coughing and scrambling away on her hands and knees, Mina grabbed the notebook and tried to make a run for it. One part of her told her to forget it, flight over fight, save her own skin. But another part needed to look, needed to see who it was that was helping her. Craning her neck, Mina saw and gasped. It was a young man who couldn't have been older than seventeen. How could she abandon him? Mina froze, but she didn't know how to help. The boy was definitely overpowered and outweighed, but he looked determined.

Wolf man lunged, and the boy feinted to the right and sidestepped; turning, he spun his body into the older, stronger man and was able to land a side kick to his solar plexus. Grunting, wolf man lowered his head and pretended to lower his guard. The dark-haired boy ran and was going to kick him in the face, but the man lunged forward, snapping his jaws very similarly to a real wolf, and knocked the boy out of the air as if he were swatting a fly.

The boy landed on the ground and tried to roll, but the wolf man was everywhere, and soon he was trapped within reach of the man's huge forearms.

The man laughed evilly and grabbed the boy around his chest, lifting him into the air, hoping to crush him.

"Use the book!" the boy yelled.

"What?" Mina asked.

"Turn the page." He was struggling and losing the fight. "Think of something you're scared of."

Grabbing the notebook, which had landed open, she flipped the page as a childhood fear flashed through her mind. She gasped as a bright light flooded the alley and the notebook grew warm to the touch. A loud buzzing noise grew in volume. Mina dropped the notebook as golden bees of light flew out of the book and straight for the man with the wolf tattoo. It looked to be painful, because he hollered and fell backward, crawling away from the bees. A few more whimpers followed, and then he gave up and ran out of the alley, the light diminishing after him.

Mina looked in surprise at the boy, who was bent over, catching his breath. "Grey Tail will be back—there's no question about that. You need to be more careful." The boy looked Mina over. "What was fate thinking, choosing you? And BEES? Really? That was the best you could come up with?

Mina turned to look at the boy. "What are you talking about?" she nearly cried, her voice raised in anxiety. "Who are you? Who's Grey Tail, and how do you know about the book?"

"Doesn't matter," he said, shrugging. "We all know about the book. All you need to know is that I'm here now, and he's gone." The boy put his hands in his pockets and didn't make any move to come closer to Mina. She looked him over head to toe.

Mina took a few steps back away from the boy. "That's not good enough. I'm in charge of protecting this, and I need to know who you are and how you found me."

The young man looked at Mina warily and said, "Don't worry, girl. I have no interest in the Grimoire. Or in you."

Mina's mouth opened and closed in obvious shock. She had never been treated with such disdain—okay, maybe once or twice at school, but never from a perfect stranger.

"So you know about the Grimoire?"

"More than I want to," he said, his lip curled in contempt. He began to walk away, but Mina realized he might be her only chance at getting some answers.

"Wait! Are you a Grimm, too?

He laughed. "Not on your life."

"Then who are you?"

"Maybe you shouldn't be asking who, but *what*." He paused and looked at her.

An otherworldly chill ran over Mina's skin, and she swallowed nervously. "Okay, then *what* are you?"

He smiled and crossed his arms in front of his chest. "Now that would be too easy, wouldn't it? I suppose you'll have to guess."

"Can't you just tell me? I don't have time to play twenty questions," Mina asked, surprised at the desperation in her voice. The boy obviously knew the man with the wolf tattoo and about the family curse.

"I could, but I won't." He raised his head and grinned like a know-it-all. "You're on your own, sweetie."

"Well, that's just rude," Mina said, putting her hands on her hips. "Why'd you show up here in the first place?"

"No, rude is not saying thank you."

Mina blinked taken aback. Was he being mean to her only because she didn't say thank you? "I'm sorry, you're right. Thank you for saving me."

The boy looked only slightly appeased. "It doesn't mean as much if I have to remind you." He turned his head, and his dark hair flew over his eyes in a rakish manner. He was remarkably good-looking, with dark somber gray eyes and a perfectly formed jaw. Thin, but with strong shoulders and a graceful stance.

"You won't last a week," the boy said to her now, his eyes studying her. "The first tale that the Story throws your way will be the end of you."

"I could, if you helped me."

He shook his head slowly in response, then turned his back to her and began to walk away. Mina reached for his shoulder, and he spun around almost instantly. One minute they were standing in the middle of the alley, and the next he had her pinned against a brick wall, his hand around her neck.

"Do not touch me!" he growled out between clenched teeth.

Mina knew she should be afraid, but she wasn't. "Why won't you help me?" she pleaded, daring to stare him in the eyes.

"I. Can't."

"Can't, or won't?"

"Both." He let go of her, and Mina slid down the wall to land on her knees in the dirt. "Can't because you're in over your head, won't because you're a lost cause. So you're not worth the effort. Today proved that." He stepped back and looked at Mina, crouched in the dirt.

Tears fell freely down her cheeks. He was confirming her worst fears, but she had to survive. "You're wrong."

"I'm never wrong," the boy answered, kneeling down to look at her closely.

"You have to be. I have to break the curse. I have to finish the tales!"

"Why? What's in it for you? What have they promised you that would make you so determined to risk your life?"

"What are you talking about? I haven't been promised anything! I'm trying to protect my brother, Charlie. He's too young. I won't let him be the next victim." Mina gritted it out, her fingers digging into the ground in anger.

It was one of the first times in her life that Mina had ever felt this angry. She was usually the passive-aggressive student who avoided confrontation, but it was as if something in her had been broken and would never be the same. "I will survive–I will be the Grimm to finish the tales and live. I will beat the Story." Mina stood and looked heatedly in his eyes. "With or without your help." With strength that Mina didn't know she had, she pushed the boy in the chest so hard he stumbled backward but did not fall.

The boy stepped away from Mina, giving her room to pass. He cocked his head to the side and answered, "Well, maybe there is a chance for you after all."

"Leave me alone!" Mina yelled, and turned angrily to face him, but the boy had disappeared.

Mina ran the rest of the way home and burst through the door to find Nan sitting on her couch, eyes red from crying. Nan flew to Mina and grabbed her around the neck.

"You're alive. I'm so sorry—I should never have left your side. I went outside to look for a number, and as soon as I turned around, the door, window, everything was gone. It was a brick wall." Nan stepped back away from Mina, and her hands went into overdrive as she explained what happened. "I went into the pottery store and asked them about the building, and they gave me a blank stare. Apparently there has never been a shop there. Same with Rosie's Flowers. Mina, they thought I was crazy, but I knew better. I knew that the building was there and it had eaten you!" She hiccupped with anxiety.

"Nan, I'm fine," Mina consoled her best friend, getting her to sit on the couch once again.

"I waited. I waited on the sidewalk for hours, but you never appeared. I searched the whole block and alley for you, and I couldn't find you." Nan began to cry. "I didn't know what else to do but to come back and wait for you. I'm just glad your mom and brother weren't here. I wouldn't want to explain to them how you were eaten by a building." Nan's hands flew through the air with her growing anxiety. When she had a moment to settle down, she pinned Mina with a wary glance. "What did happen to you?"

"I found the Grimoire." Mina smiled widely and pulled out the red spiral notebook to show Nan.

Nan frowned at the notebook. "That sure doesn't look like a Grimoire. But then again, how should I know?"

"It was in that building, I had to solve a few puzzles to find it, deep underground. But it was like it wanted me to find it. You wouldn't believe it."

"May I?" Nan asked, pointing to the cover. When Mina nodded, Nan gently opened the cover and began flipping through the pages. "Okay. There's only one story inside."

"What! That wasn't there a minute ago." Mina pointed to the pages. "There were pictures and stories, but then it erased itself when I took hold of it. And now this. What do you think it means?"

"That it's obviously not complete? That the Grimm brothers never made it through all of the stories? But I guess they finished this bull story."

"Give me that!" Mina snatched the book from Nan. "Nan, this is the room I was describing. It's all here, everything. Even me running from the room!"

"Way cool. Am I in there?"

"Nan, you know what this means?" Mina said, ignoring her. "I solved one of the tales. It's officially begun."

"Great! Now how many more until you're done?"

"Um, I don't actually know."

"Mina?" Nan asked. "What if there is no end?"

CHAPTER 12

The next day Mina went through the motions of paying attention in class, but her mind was a million miles elsewhere, Nan's words still ringing in her head: "What if there is no end?" Mina kept checking the Grimoire to make sure the story was still there. It wasn't until advanced art that she felt another trickle of dread. Something was wrong. People were whispering and pointing.

Looking up, Mina was surprised to see a set of familiar grey eyes staring at her from across the room. It was the same boy who saved her in the alley, here in their classroom and addressing their art teacher. Mr. Ames gestured for the boy to take up an empty seat.

"Class, this is Jared. He's one of our newest students. Please make him feel at home."

Mina saw the girls and boys in her class whispering among themselves. It so happened that one of the only empty seats was next to her desk, so she tried to compose herself as Jared sat down, knowing all eyes were pointed their way.

"What are you doing here?" she hissed when no was looking.

"Free country. Isn't it?" Jared said.

Mina fumed. Why was he torturing her? Lucky for her, advanced art class was less lecture and more practical study, so she had time to sort through her thoughts.

When Mr. Ames announced the first assignment, she ignored Jared, stood up, and walked across the room to sit by one of the potter's wheels. Mina loved how a pile of clay could be manipulated and formed on a wheel into something useful and pretty. She tore off a hunk of wet clay and dropped it onto the center of the wheel, reaching down to turn the power on. Getting her hands wet, she felt the pull of the clay and centered it on the wheel so it could begin to take shape.

"What are you making?" Jared asked, taking a seat at the next empty potter's wheel. He, too, picked up a lump of red clay and began the process of centering it.

"Are you here to harass me?" she asked.

"No. I'm here to make a vase," he replied tartly.

Mina sneaked a glance, and was actually surprised at how deftly his hands moved over the clay. But, still irritated from the other night, she ignored him.

"You know you can't ignore me forever," he said. His hands moved as if they were in tune with the clay.

"Watch me," Mina answered from between clenched teeth.

"It wasn't an impolite question. I'm trying to carry on a civil conversation with you."

"There's nothing civil about you, and I would prefer to not carry this conversation any further." Mina grunted in protest as she took her eyes off the wheel to confront Jared. Her mound of clay became unbalanced and flopped over to the side.

"That's too bad," he replied. "You should never let distractions get in the way of your goals. It always leads to misfortune."

"You want to know what I'm making?" Mina asked. "Here." She stopped the wheel and hit the lopsided clump with her fist. "It's an ashtray." She scooped the piece up, threw it back into the clay bucket, and walked out of the classroom, stopping at the nearest bathroom to wash the red clay from her hands and nails.

She wondered what had come over her, but something about that boy had gotten under her skin. His unwillingness to be truthful with her, for one thing. Mina didn't bother returning to her art class, knowing that she had enough finished pieces to pass the quarter. Mr. Ames was pretty lenient when it came to art. He never felt that the artist should be stifled, so they were allowed to come and go as they pleased as long as they had enough projects to pass.

Mina waited until the bell rang and practically flew toward Nan's locker. "Nan, he's here."

Nan put her books away and looked at Mina. "Who's here?"

"The boy from the alley." She had told Nan about him in two short and stiff sentences over the weekend.

"No way!" Nan held up her phone to Mina. "Is this him? I've been getting texts about him ever since he walked through the school doors. My, he is cute, isn't he?" She leaned over and looked into her locker mirror, and pressed her lips together to apply more gloss. Today she wore an Aerosmith T-shirt and bottle-cap belt, her soft blonde hair flowing in waves just past her shoulders. No matter what outfit or ensemble Nan wore, she was always beautiful.

Mina thought for a second. "I guess he is kind of cute. And if he weren't so rude, you probably would like him."

Nan and Mina walked toward the lunchroom, and Mina was secretly relieved to see that she was not the center of attention. Nan pulled on Mina's jacket to lead her over to their usual table, but Mina froze when she saw Jared was already sitting there.

Mina pulled away from Nan, and went and sat by Brody and his friends, who looked at her in surprise. Nan followed glumly and sat down, too. Disappointed she didn't get to meet the hot new guy, Nan was quickly appeased when Justin from the water polo team started flirting with her.

"I'm glad that you're okay." Brody leaned over to Mina and whispered so only she could hear. "I've been worried about you. I waited for you, and you never showed up. I've been tearing myself to pieces with worry."

"Nothing to be worried about. See, I'm fine." Mina gestured to her body, that she was in fact whole and in one piece.

Brody stared at her face and the faint outline of the bruise on her cheek. Her makeup had done a good job of covering up most of the yellowness, but it had started to fade. Her hand flew to her cheek reflexively when she noticed his stare.

"Does it hurt?" he asked.

"Not anymore. Like I told you, I'm fine."

"Is that why you didn't come to school?"

"There would have been too many awkward questions. It was easier to stay home."

Brody nodded in understanding "What did you tell your mom?"

"Nothing yet. I have nothing new to tell her."

Brody stiffened. Mina could tell he was angry that she hadn't told her mother. "Why not?"

"It would make her worry."

"She should be worried. You should be worried!" He spoke in a clipped manner.

"Brody, if you're going to start this argument again, then I'll find somewhere else to sit." Mina turned to get up.

"No, wait. I won't bring it up again." Brody reached out and grabbed her arm. "I'm just glad you're safe."

She licked her lips nervously. "Thanks to you. I'm sorry for the way that I acted."

"No," Brody interrupted. "I shouldn't have pressured you into going to the police. I'm just glad you're okay. I've been worried sick, since I had no way to call you and you didn't come to school."

Mina could feel Jared's eyes studying her from across the lunchroom, so she continued to talk to Brody. For some reason this seemed to upset Jared, and she could tell even from a distance that he glowered. It was funny to see her and Nan's usually empty table now filled with girls vying for Jared's attention and boys trying to assess their competition. But he still managed to shoot her dark looks that made her skin crawl.

Lunch flew by, and Mina was dismayed to find that Jared was in two more of her classes. How had he managed it, when Nan couldn't even get her schedule to follow Mina's? Thankfully, he didn't try to start any more conversations with her. Maybe it was because Mina kept glaring at him and holding up her textbook like it was the Great Wall of China.

It was during the last period of the day, right before the bell rang, that he finally spoke up again.

"You didn't bring it, did you?" he asked in a whisper.

"Bring what?" Mina kept her eyes glued to the sentence she was reading, even though she had already read it ten times. She had been unable to study since he sat down.

"You know what. Tell me you brought it." He actually looked a little panicked that she might not have it with her.

"No, I didn't." Mina glared at him. "I was almost attacked and killed because I had it. I'm not going to carry it around with me everywhere. I wouldn't be safe."

Jared's face became stiff, and his jaw clenched in anger. "You're not safe without it."

"What do you care? I'm not supposed to live past the end of the week, remember? Your exact words." Thankfully, the bell rang, and Mina stood up and stomped out of the classroom, leaving an opened-mouth Jared in her wake. He called her name, but she ignored him.

She made a beeline for her locker and was actually hoping that Brody had forgiven her and was waiting by it; thankfully, he was. Mina grinned as he reached over to grab her bag from her. *A girl could really get used to this,* she thought. She was so preoccupied on the drive home that she didn't even notice when Brody drove right to her front door.

"How did know where I live?" she asked quietly.

Brody nodded toward the Golden Palace and the mural of articles plastered with Mina's face, the Wongs' way of advertising that they rented to the town hero. "I did my own investigation. So you live in a Chinese restaurant?" Brody asked, his cheeks dimpling with uncontained mirth.

Mina's own cheeks burned with embarrassment. "No, I live *above* a Chinese restaurant. Big difference, believe me." She laughed hesitantly at her own lame joke.

Brody leaned away from the car, hands in his pockets. "Either way, I'm jealous. I love Chinese food."

"You should try their pot stickers sometime. They are to die for," Mina answered casually.

"Sounds good. It's a date, then." He walked to the Golden Palace, opened the door, and motioned for her to go in.

"I didn't ask...er, I wasn't implying that we should." She stumbled on her words.

Brody smiled. "I know you didn't. I did. I'm taking you out on a date. A real date, not just drive-through burgers."

"I don't know if that's such a good idea." Mina felt as if her world was collapsing in on her. Could this be real? Or some impossible fairy tale dreamt up by the Story? Either way, she didn't want it to end.

Brody paused at the entrance to the Golden Palace to study the crudely placed pictures and articles about Mina taped to the glass. He looked from the paper clippings to Mina and back. "You know, those pictures don't do you justice."

Mina pushed him farther into the restaurant and away from the newspaper mural. Mrs. Wong waved excitedly and motioned for them to take a seat. Mina didn't know what to do with her hands, so she kept fidgeting with the chopsticks on the table. By the time Mrs. Wong brought them over some ice waters, Mina's nerves were so taut that she knocked over her ice water on the table, some spilling into Brody's lap.

"I'm so sorry!" Mina began pulling napkins out of the dented holder and flung them at Brody. She was so distressed that she accidentally pulled the casing off the napkin holder, which flew across the floor and spun to a stop by a wide-eyed Mrs. Wong.

Brody jumped up and began dabbing calmly at his thighs. When the table no longer looked like Niagara Falls, he excused himself to go clean up in the bathroom, laughing the whole way.

Mina groaned and pounded her forehead against the table repeatedly.

Mrs. Wong stormed up to the table to voice her opinion as soon as Brody left. "OOOHHH, he a hottie, that one. Meehna, you keep that one for sure, bring him by more often! I will get lots of business."

Mina tried to look at Mrs. Wong, but a piece of napkin from the wet table was stuck to Mina's forehead, obscuring her view. "You have got to be kidding. I doubt he will ever be seen in public with me again. I'm a walking, talking catastrophe."

Mrs. Wong snatched the napkin from Mina's forehead and started waving it in the air at her while she lectured Mina. "You leesten to me. He nice boy, will forgive real quick with kissy." Mrs. Wong raised her eyebrows and bobbed her head at Mina encouragingly.

Mina groaned and pounded her head against the table again. When Brody came back, they ordered and sat silently while Mrs. Wong kept filling their bowls with all-you-can-eat pot stickers.

"You're right, these are to die for." Brody took another bite. "But does she always hover like this?" Brody cocked his head to a smiling Mrs. Wong, who continued to make smooching faces whenever he turned his back.

"Um, no. I think they changed the dose on her meds," Mina lied, trying desperately not to look in Mrs. Wong's direction. Pretty soon her husband came out in his white apron and joined in the charade of advice. His wife must have told him about Mina's embarrassing spectacle, because he shook his head in his wife's direction and mimed dropping a napkin on the floor. Both of them were miming different actions, perhaps trying to get Mina to crack.

Mina kept shaking her head "no" in their direction. When Brody saw Mina's head shake and looked over his shoulder, the couple finally dropped their act and began furiously cleaning the counters. As soon as he turned back, they went at it again.

"You ready to get out of here?" Mina asked desperately, looking over Brody's shoulder.

Brody threw some money on the table while Mina stared daggers at the laughing couple, and they escaped into the crisp afternoon air.

They started walking the different districts with no particular destination in mind. Mina knew they needed to discuss what happened the other night, but she wasn't sure she was ready. She'd found the Grimoire, but she didn't know how Jared or the man with the wolf tattoo figured in, and she was running out of ideas. But she didn't know if she could trust Brody.

As if reading her mind, Brody spoke up. "You know you can talk to me, right? I'm here for you."

Mina kicked a stray piece of rock with her shoe. "How can I, when I barely know you?"

"I'm trying to amend that," he said softly. He brought his hand down and cupped her small hand in his. Mina tried to pull away, but he held on. "I'm sorry that I pressured you into going to the police after what happened, but you have to understand I was scared for you. I wanted to protect you."

Mina shook her head, but Brody continued, "You're right—I don't know what's going on. But I want to help you. I want to be there for you."

"I can't talk about it. I'm not ready to talk about it. I'm still trying to figure things out. But when I know more, when I'm ready, I'll tell you." It was the most she could promise.

They headed down the hill to the river walk, and Brody bought some bread to feed the geese in the river. Mina couldn't help but glare at the geese angrily and refused to throw them bread.

"You got a grudge against geese?" Brody joked.

"You bet I do. Stupid birds." Mina snorted. She was boycotting all geese for leading her into danger. Now, even though Mina wasn't the one throwing the bread or even holding it, the geese waddled out of the river and seemed to be pecking their way toward her. Mina jumped back and kept walking backward, but it was as if they had heard her call them stupid. They kept following her until Mina stumbled and landed on her butt in the grass.

Screaming, Mina held up her hands as the swarm of geese started to crawl over her.

"Get out of here. Scram!" Brody yelled, kicking and pushing the flock away from Mina. Reaching down, he grabbed her arm and pulled her up and out of the reach of the geese. The geese kept following. Laughing, Brody physically lifted Mina up out of their reach and over his shoulder like a sack of potatoes. Mina's feet swung in the air, her hair hanging over her face upside down. Brody moved away from the river and away from the attacking flock.

He turned around to look at the geese and burst out laughing. The whole gaggle diligently followed them in a "V" formation. "I think you underestimate these geese. They are definitely not stupid." Brody laughed.

"They are, too. Put me down!" Mina cried out, hitting Brody's back playfully.

"No way, not until you're out of danger. I won't abandon you again." He held on tighter, walking faster.

Mina rolled her eyes at the geese, which never actually bit her but certainly startled her. She tried making shooing motions over Brody's shoulder, to no avail. Finally she whispered between clenched teeth, "If you don't get lost now, there won't be a happy ending. I happen to be friends with a restaurant owner who would love some fresh goose."

The geese immediately turned and headed back to the river. Mina stared in amazement, while Brody, realizing that the threat was over, put Mina down. "That was the strangest thing I've ever seen."

Mina snorted. "Not for me."

"Are there a lot of strange things that happen around you?"

"Haven't you noticed I'm cursed?" Mina meant the words as a joke, but as soon as they left her mouth, she felt a tingle of apprehension through her bones. The words were too close to the truth.

Brody shook his head. They spent the evening on the river walk, watching the different street performers and musicians entertain guests. "I've never been down here before."

"It's like the wrong side of the tracks for your kind."

"What do you mean by 'my kind'?" Brody stopped and looked at Mina carefully.

"Well, you know…" She shrugged.

"No, I don't know."

"The rich kind."

Brody rolled his eyes. "Mina, you don't get it. I don't care about money or fame or social status. I would rather have been born without it. My family is hardly ever home because of it. My friends are only my friends because they think that I can do something for them. Everyone is always watching me, judging me, trying to see if I'm going to fit into the box they want me in, whether it's spoiled rich kid or reckless heir. In a way, being rich is its own curse."

Mina pondered his words, letting them sink in. They were both the same in many ways. "I'm sorry, Brody. You're right."

"No, don't apologize. I mean, I was that person, for a while. I was what money had made me into, but not anymore. I'm trying to change. I'm trying to be worthy of you."

Mina blanched in surprise. "Funny. I feel like it's the other way around. I feel like I need to pinch myself, or wake up from whatever dream I'm in, because I can't understand why you want to be my friend."

"You really don't get it, do you?" Brody turned Mina toward him and held tightly onto her shoulders. "I don't want to be your friend."

CHAPTER 13

Mina felt her stomach drop into her shoes. She looked at the ground in dismay. She knew this was too good to be true. She tried to turn away, but Brody gripped her shoulders harder. She looked up in surprise just as Brody kissed her gently on the forehead. "I want to be more."

Mina felt her knees go weak, and for once had no snappy retort.

"But I have a feeling, if I pressure you, you're going to run for the hills," Brody continued. "So I'm willing to wait until you're ready." He had pulled her into a hug and was whispering into her soft brown hair. "See you're already shaking." He pulled away from her, and she felt an immediate sense of loss. That one brief moment had felt...right.

Mina sighed wistfully, but didn't feel totally abandoned, as Brody continued to hold her hand. He walked her up the stairs to the door of her flat. Mina fumbled for the key and dropped it. She reached down sheepishly and was about to insert it when the door opened on its own.

"That's strange," Mina said, leaning past Brody and pushing the door further open until it finally hit something solid. The little view they had through the opened door was enough to make Mina's heart race with fear. Their kitchen was destroyed.

Panicking, Mina pushed on the door harder, but it didn't budge. Sensing her fear, Brody helped her push and got the door open, but grabbed Mina's arm just as she was about to run headlong into danger. A chair had been knocked over in front of the door.

Brody shook his head and held up one finger to his mouth. He entered first, silently, and moved through each room, looking behind curtains, under beds, and in the closets. When he was sure it was safe, he motioned for Mina to enter her family's apartment.

The sparse furnishings were knocked over, dumped out, and looked to have been rummaged through, but nothing was actually damaged too badly. When you didn't own a lot, a thorough search wouldn't actually take too long.

"No one's here."

Mina needed to see for herself. She followed the same steps Brody took and noticed nothing was terribly wrong. She could probably put her home to rights before her family got home. She was about to enter her bedroom, but Brody stopped her.

"Mina, it doesn't look too bad except for that room. It's been destroyed."

Mina peeked into her own bedroom and felt her cheeks burn with embarrassment. It looked exactly the same as before, except her dresser drawers had been left open, with clothes hanging out. But Mina wasn't about to admit it. She closed her bedroom door and walked back to the kitchen, and began to put drawers and utensils back where they belonged.

Brody went to the living room and helped pick up the potted plants, even sweeping up the dirt. Mina was secretly impressed that he hadn't once urged her to call the police. She was now doubly thankful that she had taken the Grimoire to school with her, despite what she'd told Jared.

Wait a minute. Could he have done this? she thought. Could he have followed her home and trashed her house while she was out with Brody? He knew who she was, he knew about the Grimoire, and he's specifically asked if she'd left it at home. Maybe he was in league with this Grey Tail, and simply trying to gain her trust?

Brody noticed that Mina had quit straightening and had begun to shake. He saw her, and this time she came to him willingly and buried her face in his chest. "It's okay. I'll protect you," he whispered.

Mina wished she could believe Brody, but he had no idea what she was up against. How could he protect her and her family? Mina was still wrapped up in Brody's arms when the door opened and Sara walked in, carrying brown paper grocery bags. She dropped them on the floor when she saw her daughter in the arms of an unknown boy.

Mina jumped back guiltily. Brody regretfully let her go, bending down to help her mother regain the dropped bags.

"Pardon me, Mrs. Grime." Brody deposited the bags onto the kitchen table. He turned, scooped the bag Charlie was carrying out of his hands, and picked up the cans that had escaped onto the floor before Sara could recover and close her mouth.

"And *who* are you?" Sara asked. Mina wished her mother wasn't always so suspicious.

"Brody Carmichael." He leaned forward and offered Sara his hand. "I know Mina from school."

Sara's eyes widened when she recognized the name.

"Oh, that's right. He's the boy who you lent your notes to for class. Seriously, Brody, you should learn to take your own notes and not live off the sympathy of others," Sara lectured.

Brody's eyes widened with shock. He looked over to a white-faced Mina before answering. "You are absolutely right, Mrs. Grime. But you see, if I hadn't asked to borrow your daughter's notes, I would have had no excuse to ask her on a date," he lied.

Mina could have died right then and been happy. Brody looked over at Mina with a crooked smile and raised eyebrow. He was going to ask her about this conversation later. She knew it.

Sara, however, wasn't convinced. "*And* you're the boy who ran over Mina's bike."

"Yes, unfortunately that as well. And I really couldn't be more embarrassed. But I was so surprised to see her on my front porch, I wasn't watching where I was driving. I'm trying to make up for it by giving Mina rides to and from school."

"Oh. Oh, I see." Sara smiled. "Please call me Sara. Mrs. Grime sounds old." She began putting away the groceries. "Sorry about the mix-up with the work pamphlets. My boss told me your house, and I sent Mina to drop it off. We never did figure out where the mix-up in communication was or where it was really supposed to go. But maybe it was fate." When Sara left it at that, Mina wanted to crawl under a rock and hide. She couldn't make eye contact with Brody.

Brody stayed for a supper of spaghetti and meatballs, which turned into a rather awkward event. He would direct questions toward Charlie, but when Charlie wouldn't answer, Brody would speak louder, as if he was deaf.

"He can hear you," Mina said, giving her brother a sisterly kick under the table. "He just doesn't talk."

Charlie tried to hide his smile but couldn't. He had enjoyed tormenting Brody.

All through dinner, Brody gave Mina pointed stares, looking around the kitchen in an effort for her to tell her mom what had happened. But Mina kept trying to mouth words like "not yet," or "not now."

But Brody apparently wasn't going to let it slide. "Do you feel safe here, Sara?"

Mina could have kicked him if she'd had long enough legs.

"Why, yes, of course I do. What would make you say that?" Sara asked.

"It's just that you're here all alone in an older section of town, with two kids. I was just wondering if you ever felt like you were endangering them by living here in the international district."

"What kind of question is that?" Sara asked heatedly.

Brody's jaw tightened in anger. "I'm trying to protect your daughter, but she doesn't seem to think she is in any danger." Brody put it all on the table and looked to Mina in challenge. Mina knew then that if she didn't tell her mother now, Brody would.

"Mom, you know that family thing that we discovered last week? The one where I would most likely face certain obstacles and you agreed to let me try?" Mina tried to hint; she didn't want to alarm her younger brother or give Brody to much information.

"Yes?" Sara spoke warily, her eyes darting worriedly between Brody and Charlie.

"Well, someone was looking for something that I didn't have. They confronted me outside a library last week, and two days ago in an alley, and it seems they were here in our house just a few hours ago."

"WHAT?" Brody and Sara said in unison. Brody didn't know that Mina had been attacked in an alley.

Sara looked at Brody. "What? You didn't know?"

"Not about all of it. I knew about the library, because I was there, but not about another attack in the alley. It's why I was asking about your safety." Brody had started speaking in the vague way Mina did, in an effort to protect Charlie as well.

"I see." Sara sat down calmly at the table and tried to compose herself. Charlie watched his mother quietly. Sara leaned over and whispered to Charlie, who brightened at her comment, ran to the freezer and took out a gallon of ice cream, and went to his room. When Charlie's door was shut and the sound of cartoons could be heard from behind the door, Sara turned to look at Brody.

He spoke before she could. "Are you two in some kind of trouble? Are there people after you? What can I do to help you?" Brody stood up and paced the kitchen.

Sara continued eating her dinner and wiped her mouth daintily with her napkin. "This really is a family matter, Brody. But don't worry—we haven't done anything illegal, and I won't let anyone harm my daughter ever again. I've moved across country six times to protect Mina from what is after her, and I'm prepared to move continents if I have to."

Brody froze at her words. "You know what's after her, and you haven't gone to the police?" He turned on Sara. "If what you're saying is true, then the police can find the person. They can stop this man."

"I told you, this is a family matter."

Brody looked to Mina in a panic. "I won't let you run, not if I can help you. If you will just let me help you…"

Sara pretended he'd directed his question at her. "Can you help us run from a curse?"

"What? I don't understand," Brody began, but Sara cut him off.

"Brody, you've spent two years at the same school as Mina, hardly talking to her, never even realizing she is alive. Then she goes and does something crazy, against my wishes.

She placed her own life in danger to save yours." Her face became very still. "Now, because of those actions, our whole family has to live with the consequences. You now feel obligated to help her, like she did you. I get that, I really do. But what gives you the right to question our actions and lifestyle?"

Silence filled the kitchen. Mina held her breath, afraid to move. Brody straightened in his seat and swallowed slowly.

Sara brushed her hands over her forehead in defeat. "You're enamored, that's it. In another week or so, you will wake up, and this will all be a dream. You will forget that Mina ever even saved your life. She will go back to being my clumsy, forgotten, outcast teen daughter, and you will go back to ruling the school and dating the head cheerleader."

Silent tears fell down Mina's cheeks. How could her mother say these things? Mina refused to look at either of them, staring at her plate of uneaten pasta and letting her mother's words, words she knew were the truth, sink in. She could have stopped her mother, but Mina knew that Sara was only protecting her.

Sara pointed her fork at Brody accusingly, a giant meatball stuck on the end. "I've seen it all before. This will fade—it won't last, and you will leave Mina for another. We aren't like you people. You two are oil and water. But how we live our life is of no concern to you or your family. My daughter doesn't challenge your choices or way of life, so don't do it to us. You haven't earned that right or proven yourself worthy." Once Sara had her say, she set her fork down and began slicing the meatball into bite-sized pieces. Placing a piece in her mouth, she chewed slowly, challenging Brody with her eyes.

Mina was stunned at how well Brody took the news. He listened and never once questioned Sara's sanity, maybe because it was her mother, and not Mina herself, who was explaining things to him.

Instead he was quiet, contemplative. "That explains a lot," he said finally. Brody stood and excused himself from the dinner table. "Thank you for dinner and an enlightening evening, Sara. Mina." Brody nodded his head in both their directions and let himself out the front door.

"What just happened, Mom?" Mina asked. Her lip began quivering, tears flowing freely. Her heart felt like it had been ripped in two.

"I think you've just been dumped."

CHAPTER 14

Sara looked at her daughter, who was clearly devastated, and immediately adopted a softer tone. "I'm so sorry, honey. I judged him wrong. I thought he could handle the challenge of the truth, that he could even be the one."

"What do you mean, Mom, 'the one'? I don't want 'the one,' just a boyfriend."

"That's not your fate, Mina. Anyone you're not serious about – and even those you are serious about – are going to get hurt. Think about it. Fairy tales time and time again tend to have a hero who will battle it to the end to save the heroine. I was hoping he would fight for you more, challenge me, tell me I was wrong and be your knight, like your father was for me. But I misjudged him. I'm sorry." Sara tried to put her hand on Mina's, but Mina jerked it away.

"Just...leave me alone. For a little while. Can you least do that for me, after you drove him away?"

Mina tried to ignore her mother's hurt expression and went to the living room window, peering out to the street below. Sure enough, Brody's car was gone. Still silently crying, Mina went to the front door, locked it, and put a chair in front of the handle. She then went to every window, checked and locked all of them. Going to her bedroom, Mina grabbed a throw blanket, opened her window, and crawled up the fire escape to the roof.

The roof was Mina's one retreat from the world. As the only tenant in the small building, Mina had the space all to herself and could lavish the roof with fun items, her own personal touch. Since it was twilight, she went to a small electrical outlet and switched on the power, illuminating the small space with strands of white Christmas lights and various illuminated patio lights. Last summer Mina had dragged up two lawn chairs and had even planted fake plastic flowers in all the planters.

Italian music played softly from a restaurant down the street, and Mina collapsed in a lawn chair. Wrapping herself in the blanket, Mina watched as steam rose from various vents and chimneys across the building's roofs. She cried herself to sleep, unaware of the eyes that watched her.

CHAPTER 15

Mina spent the next morning avoiding everyone, and trying unsuccessfully to transfer her classes with the school office. It would mean giving up homeroom with Nan, but Mina was desperate. She didn't think she could stomach Brody's betrayal and Jared's discord at the same time and survive. She had looked for Brody's car on the way to school and in the parking lot, but didn't see it. He wasn't even at lunch. Mina pushed her food around on her tray and waited for Nan to join her.

Along with feeling guilty and depressed, Mina had opened her locker to find another note. Quite a few, actually; her locker was stuffed with them. Some said LOSER, FAKE, GOLD DIGGER, but the one that scared her most was the one written in red ink.

I KNOW WHO YOU ARE! YOU'RE DEAD!

Mina couldn't figure out what she could have done to cause this kind of discord. She had tried to live a quiet and unnoticed life, and had been relatively successful until the school field trip. For two whole days she had been a celebrity, but after that news died down, she was back to being boring Mina. Except now someone was trying to intimidate and bully her through notes. Her best bet was to try to finish whatever tale she was in right now, and move on to the next as soon as possible. If only she could figure out what the Story wanted from her. What did she need to do to reach the ending?

She was so deep in self-pity that Mina didn't even notice when someone sat down next to her until they began talking.

"It doesn't have to be this way between us, you know." Mina looked up to see Jared leaning against the table, dressed head to toe in black with black jeans, black shoes, and a black jacket.

"I've decided that I would rather not get to know you, since you don't care enough to explain things to me or even help me. So if you're not going to do either, then you're just a thorn in my side. Now please, go sit elsewhere." Mina started to stab her chicken-fried steak with a vengeance.

Jared looked at Mina's lunch and laughed. He had a very engaging smile, which only made Mina's mood turn darker. Why should he be so cheerful when she felt so, well, grim? "Tell you what," he said. "You live out the week, and I will agree to help you."

Mina turned on him angrily. "Did you ransack my house?"

"What? No." Jared's smile fell from his face. "I did not, nor have I ever, entered your home. But I probably know who did." His dark brows furrowed in thought. "Strange, I wouldn't have thought him smart enough to try."

"Who, Jared? If you know something that could protect my family, then you need to tell me." Mina was getting more frustrated by the minute. One minute he was charming, the next minute he was as elusive and vague as the best politician.

"Grey Tail wouldn't have gone there on his own. He would have been sent by someone with enough power to sway the wolf pack." Jared looked worried.

"Wolf pack! Jared, what are you talking about?" Mina felt the hair on the back of her arms rise in fear.

She didn't get an answer to her question, because Pri and Savannah brought their trays and sat down next to Mina. They began chatting like they were long-lost friends.

Jared leaned back and watched the exchange with narrowed eyes.

"So, Mina, what do you think of the theme for this year's dance?" Savannah asked, drawing attention to her white-blonde hair by flipping it over her shoulder.

"What theme?" Mina asked, barely hiding her annoyance.

"They're calling it 'Enchanted.' We're all supposed to dress up as famous storybook characters."

"I hadn't heard, I guess. I've been pretty busy." Mina answered. She had visibly tried to not cringe when she heard the theme. How ironic was that? She had been so distracted she had forgotten completely about the dance, but then she did recall Nan texting pictures back and forth with people in possible dresses and costumes.

"So then Brody Carmichael hasn't asked you to go with him?" Savannah asked offhandedly, but her body stiffened, waiting for a reply. Mina could have sworn she saw her hold her breath.

"No, I don't dance. I've been told it's bad for my health," Mina answered casually, and watched as Savannah visibly relaxed. What she'd said was true; she had yet to attend a dance where it didn't end in a torn dress, broken shoe, or sprained ankle.

"What about you, Jared? Are you going with anyone?" Pri asked. Her loaded question hung in the air like an atom bomb; she watched Jared like a lioness waiting to go in for the kill.

"Haven't decided yet," Jared answered carefully. "I'm still getting settled in. New student, remember." It was a well-played answer, and Mina was envious of his excuse.

"Well, I am going as Rapunzel, and I could use a Prince Charming." Savannah actually preened. Mina raised her eyebrows, surprised at her brazenness.

"Rapunzel is not a good choice for you," Jared said softly. "She was too naïve, too innocent. I would peg you for someone more mature, more cunning."

"Really?" Savannah leaned forward into Jared's arm and actually purred. "Who, then, should I go as?"

Jared leaned away from her with disgust. "I would peg you as a jealous stepmother." Savannah's face turned red with anger. She was actually so mad she couldn't form words.

"Really! And what would Miss Mina be, hhmmmm? The ugly stepsister? The greedy gold digger who was after MY prince?" Savannah stepped away from the table, and Pri followed after her like the good follower she was.

Mina covered her eyes with her hands and tried to massage the headache that was beginning to plague her. "You really shouldn't have done that," Mina chastised him. "You just made my life even harder. Nice work." She stood up and left her lunch tray on the table, her fork standing at attention in the middle of her chicken-fried steak.

Walking out the double doors into the hall, Mina was surprised to see Brody coming down the corridor. Mina took off down another hall, hoping he hadn't seen her. Just seeing Brody brought back a flood of feelings that she wasn't ready to deal with. She had actually felt relieved that he hadn't shown up that day for school.

When he called her name, Mina ducked into the marked stage doors, hoping he would pass her by when he turned the corner. She quietly walked up the steps onto the stage, and sat down amongst all of the decorations the student council had started creating for the dance.

There was a tinseled park bench with lights strung around it. A giant gingerbread house stood with life-size candy, a vine-covered wishing well, and a large stone tower. Mina sat on the bench and pulled her knees up to her chest. She buried her face in her knees, gently rocking herself. She wished desperately that there was a way she could turn back time. Maybe if her mother had never signed the stupid permission form, she wouldn't have gone on the field trip. She wouldn't have saved Brody's life and would never have been noticed by the curse.

She might have made it all the way through high school without having been attacked by a stranger. With what Jared said earlier, Mina became all the more skeptical of surviving this curse, because there was a wolf pack plural, as in more of those crazy tattooed biker guys after her.

Mina thought she was alone on the stage, but the sound of a stage lever being pulled made her glance up in alarm. The stage was flooded with lights as the dance displays lit up in all of their beauty. They shone, sparkled, and dazzled Mina speechless. She actually had to cover her eyes to make out the person who triggered the lights.

A dark form walked out of the shadows and stood before Mina, tall and handsome. Mina actually shivered when she looked at Brody, feeling as if her body had gone without water for days, and here was the answer to her thirst. His blond hair and blue eyes conveyed a softness to his face above a strong, chiseled jaw. His hands were in his designer jeans' pockets as he walked casually toward her on the bench. She felt as if she was under a spell, mesmerized by his movements. Closing her eyes, she tried to block out his glorious being. Maybe if she didn't see him, he would disappear.

"Mina." Brody's voice sounded husky to Mina's ears.

"Go away," she answered weakly. Her heart thudded in her chest, and it felt like it would burst.

"I need to speak to you."

"You've done enough talking. You made your point on the whole situation last night."

"No, I didn't." Brody knelt before her and stroked the back of her feather-soft brown hair. "Mina, please hear me out." Brody reached out and wrapped his hands around her. She was so small that he was able to maneuver her so that when he sat on the bench, she was tucked across his lap. She tried to squirm at first, but Brody held onto her, nuzzling her ear, which made her freeze. "What your mother said last night…well, it scared me."

"I know. It seemed enough to scare you away." Mina tried to move away, but Brody nuzzled her again, making her freeze. It was both an intoxicating feeling and an overwhelming rush.

"Not like you think. I went home, destroyed a few classic guitars, rode my motorcycle across the county. I ended up in another state, and I still couldn't contain my thoughts. You're all I think about, and last night I had an uncontrollable rage warring within me. I want to fight this battle for you, but I know that it's not my fight. You will tell me what you're afraid of when you feel ready. Your mother's right. I have no right to judge your family. I haven't proven myself yet. And I made it worse by leaving last night the way I did. I'm sorry—I shouldn't have left."

Mina's heart soared to new heights. He hadn't run from her because he was ashamed of her or didn't see a future with her. He ran because he wanted to protect her. This time it was

Mina who felt protective of Brody. "I'm sorry that I doubted you," she said quietly. "You confuse me."

"What is there to be confused about?" Brody asked.

"I thought for sure you had ended our friendship or relationship or whatever this is." Mina looked into his deep blue eyes and felt herself begin to drown.

"So you started to build up that wall between us again. I can tell. You like to hide behind that wall, locked inside that tower." Brody cupped Mina's face and whispered softly, "I'm guess I'm going to have to work on tearing down that wall, brick…" He kissed her eyelids, "…by brick…" He kissed her pert little nose, "…by brick." Brody continued to kiss her cheeks, her chin, and finally her lips.

Mina knew it was coming but was still startled by the feel of his lips on her mouth. It was glorious, sweet, and beautiful. Mina felt herself go lightheaded with joy. When he pulled away from their gentle kiss, she felt saddened by his parting, until he placed another quick kiss on her lips. "By brick," he whispered.

***

The rest of the day at school, Mina floated along. She had never felt so wonderful, and for now, nothing, not even Jared, could ruin her mood. He noticed the change in her behavior and tried to make a comment that would rile her, but she blew it off. Everything would turn out right, because Brody was there for her. She could feel it.

Mina was supposed to meet Brody by his locker after school, and as soon as the bell rang she practically skipped down the hall toward him. But a rough hand on her elbow stopped her.

"What do you think you're doing?" She turned and wasn't the least bit surprised to see Jared on the other end of her elbow. "Let go of me." She tried to shake him off, but Jared squeezed tighter.

"Come with me and I'll tell you what you want to know."

"Why?"

He was silent.

"I can't," she said, happy to blow him off. "Brody's giving me a ride home. Maybe later?" she asked, smiling.

It was the wrong thing to say to him, because his eyes darkened dangerously. "You don't know who you're dealing with here. I was going to help you, tell you information to help you stay alive, but it seems you've picked your model boyfriend over your life." He dropped her elbow and strode away.

Mina waited ten seconds, thinking through her options, and then chased after Jared into the parking lot. He must have been expecting her, because he was already astride a black motorbike. It was sleek, exciting, and dangerous, just like Jared himself. She hesitated; was this really wise? He was holding out an extra helmet to her.

"You knew I would come, didn't you?" Mina demanded angrily. "You could have at least let me tell Brody where I'm going so he doesn't worry."

Jared shook his head. "This is a one-time deal, expiring soon." He jump-started the bike. "Like now."

Mina sighed and really wished she had a cell phone to text Brody that she wasn't in danger.

But as soon as Jared peeled out of the parking lot and sped along the road, Mina had to rethink her last thought, gripping onto Jared's waist so she wouldn't fly off the bike. Maybe she was.

CHAPTER 16

Jared sped along the interstate, and fifteen minutes later he was pulling up to Emerald Lake. He turned off the motorcycle and removed his helmet, laying it on the seat. Turning, he held out his hand for Mina's helmet as well.

"What are we doing here?" Mina asked, pulling off her backpack.

"Practicing," Jared answered.

"Practicing what?"

"How to stay alive."

Mina thought he was joking, but one look at Jared's set face, and she knew he wasn't joking. "Okay. Why now?" she had to ask.

"Why not now? Do you have anything else planned?" Mina started to open her mouth, but Jared cut her off. "I do, so it's now or never."

Annoyed, Mina followed Jared out to the water's edge. He stopped by a maple tree and broke off a short branch. Jared closed his eyes, and the stick began to glow.

Mina's eyes opened wide, and she stared in awe. She'd already figured out that he was Fae, but watching him mold and shape a branch with power was certainly impressive, and hauntingly beautiful. His eyes closed in concentration; it was almost as if he was communicating with the branch.

This was real magic, she realized, beautiful and pure. Mina smiled and looked at Jared. She didn't see the annoying boy from school. She saw someone who was ethereal and glowing

147

with power. The rush of it took her breath away, long enough for her to forget, for a moment, that she didn't entirely trust him.

Mina's smile only faded when she recognized the shape he was molding the branch into. It was a weapon, a wooden sword, much more dangerous-looking than any of Charlie's. The beautiful moment passed as Mina realized her mistake. She was miles from the nearest house, without a phone. She was with a strange boy who had powers and had just morphed a tree branch into a sword. Jared had never told her exactly whose side he was on. Once the wooden blades stopped glowing, she snapped out of her reverie and took a step away from him.

Jared just looked at her, eyebrows raised, and handed her the sword.

"What's this for?" she asked, worrying over the answer.

"It's a weapon, dummy."

"And what am I supposed to do with it?"

"You're not really that dull, are you?"

Mina stuck out her tongue in response. She swung the sword around a few times while Jared began to concentrate on a second branch.

"So where do you live? Never-Never Land?" she joked.

Jared opened one eye to address her, still concentrating on the branch. "Something like that."

"Aren't the Fae supposed to be my enemy?"

"Some of them are. Which is exactly why I brought you here."

With the second sword completed, Jared took off his shoes and stepped toward the water's edge, motioning for Mina to do the same.

"Not happening." Mina felt her blood turn cold just looking at the water.

"It's either shoes, or I wish away your clothes," he threatened. Mina jumped out of her shoes so fast, she stubbed her big toe on a tree root and had to waddle out to the lake bed like a wounded duck.

"Ouch, ouch, ouch!" she mumbled, shifting from foot to foot. When she reached the water's edge, she turned and stared at Jared, rolling her eyes impatiently. He motioned for her to step deeper into the water.

Next thing she knew, with no warning, Jared rushed Mina, quickly stabbing at her with the sword. She jumped backward and barely missed being gutted by the blade. "What the heck!" she shouted. Jared turned again and swept his foot out, catching her behind the knee, and she fell backward into the water. Cold liquid burned her lungs as she inhaled the water. Mina flailed her arms and got on her knees, and crawled to the edge and began coughing.

"Why'd you do that!" she shouted.

"Relax, it's only water," he said. "You're not letting your instincts guide you. Let go of your fear, and I'll show you how to do what I just did."

Once she'd caught her breath, they started again. He taught her blocks, stabs, and even a few basic flipping moves. Obviously, most of the time he was flipping her into the water, and she came up looking like a drowned duck. Finally, Jared let Mina use a hip throw and throw him into the lake. Mina screamed and ran around in circles with her hands in the air, chanting her name and doing a victory dance.

Jared grinned and waded out of the water and over to their shoes. Carefully, he looked for dead and fallen tree limbs, and made a fire on the beach, using a lighter. Mina felt a little disappointed that he couldn't call up fire on the spot with magic. But she forgot all about her disappointment when the heat began to warm her soaked clothes.

Jared sat next to her and began what would be a very enlightening lesson. "Now, there are various Fae tale creatures that you will most definitely come across. You've already met one of the wolves."

"Don't you mean fairy tale people, not creatures? What I saw was a man, not a wolf."

"Don't let your eyes fool you. You only see what's on this plane, not the next."

"You mean there's more than one?" she asked.

Jared rolled his eyes at her question. "Of course there is more than one plane. For instance, there is the physical plane and spiritual plane. Where the physical and spiritual planes meet and the veil between the two is thinner, weaker, and constantly moving exists the Fae plane. Never-Never Land, as you say. This is where the Story itself resides and all of the Fae Tales originate. The two planes almost never converge, but when they do, the merging of the spiritual and physical creates apexes, or gates, for the Fae to cross over. Over the years, hundreds of Fae have crossed over and have run amok among the human world."

"Do you mean like fairies and witches?" Mina asked.

"Your world drew them like moths to flame. The Grimm brothers realized this. Somehow the brothers found a gate to the Fae plane and confronted the ruling Fae, or, as some call them, Fates. The Grimms demanded that the Fae return to their own plane. Now, the Fae love games more than anything, and they take great pleasure in toying with humans."

"Well, that much is obvious," she said.

"Touché," Jared replied, winking at her. "But the older ones, that's who you need to worry about. They love to feed off human emotions and energy. It's addicting to them, like the purest kind of drug.

"You can imagine, these older beings weren't about to return to their own world easily. But the Fae also love stories. So a challenge was issued to the brothers: If they could complete a list of quests based on their favorite stories, then the Fae would be drawn back to their own world and the gates closed forever. If they didn't, then the gates would stay open.

"The brothers discussed at length what to do, for the quests were numerous. They couldn't possibly achieve all of them in their lifetime. So they agreed, on the condition that if they couldn't finish the quests, then the next of their bloodline would be given a chance."

"It sounds too easy," Mina commented.

"It was, of course, but the ruling Fates were crafty. Fae can't lie, you know. But they can, and do, manipulate the truth."

"What's the difference?" Mina asked.

"Like, if you asked me if you were ugly, I couldn't say yes, but I might tell you that you'll probably never be prom queen."

"Pfft. Like I'd want to be."

"Only if Brody Carmichael were king."

Mina threw a stick at him, feeling the heat rush into her face.

"Mina, what I'm saying is, the Fates tricked your great ancestors. What the brothers didn't know was that the quests would start over from the beginning if the chosen Grimm couldn't complete them."

"But that's not fair! I shouldn't have to be shouldered with their unfinished business. My family wouldn't be cursed if they were able to finish where the others left off. The gate could have been closed long ago, and I would still have my father! I HATE this. I hate the Fae!" Mina let out a frustrated growl.

Jared's eyes darkened at her words, and Mina pinched her lips closed in remorse.

"Yes, the Fae are crafty. They don't want the gates closed. It means their playground would be off limits and they couldn't toy with the humans. So the Fae continually try to impede the Grimms' progress. They learned to hide their essence between planes and appear human, normal. But if you were able to see onto the next plane, you would see them for what they really are."

"You mean I would see that Grey Tail isn't human."

Jared nodded. "Grey Tail is very much a Fae wolf, and like all wolves, they do run in packs."

Mina shivered and rubbed her hands together over the fire.

"And what do you look like on the next plane?"

"Imagine me now, except twice as handsome."

"Yeah, right." Mina smiled for a moment, but the thought of facing others like Grey Tail truly scared her. Swallowing, she tried to regain focus on what Jared was saying. The clue to beating the curse lay somewhere with him, she knew it. "So what about the Story? You, my mother, everyone keeps referring to the Story as if it's a living, breathing thing."

"It wasn't at first, but it is now. And it's very dangerous."

"I don't understand."

"Well, when the ruling Fates set forth the quests for Jacob and Wilhelm Grimm, they kept a record of the tales on the Fae plane as their way to keep an eye on the brothers' progress. I told you the Fae love stories, and they loved to read the completed tales as the brothers finished each one. But anything that resides within the Fae plane that long eventually gains power, and it did. It became self-aware, a Fae in its own right, known as the Story. It liked the attention it was receiving from the Fae, so the Story began to interfere on its own and set up the tales for the Grimm descendants as a way to gain more power."

"It doesn't sound real. This sounds made up." Mina bit the inside of her cheek.

"Believe me, I know how unbelievable it is. Over the years the Story grew on its own. It became obsessed with re-creating the Fae tales, even forcing the occupants to participate so it could grow more powerful."

"And the ruling Fates don't care?"

"Hardly. The Fates became bored after the Grimm brothers passed on and cared little about their descendants. Few were entertaining enough for them. They...petered out too quickly. Maybe if someone came close to breaking what you call the Grimm curse, they might peek their head out of the throne room and look, but not likely."

"Did my father know all of this?" she asked.

"No."

"Why not?"

"Because he didn't ask for help."

"And I did? When did I ask for help?"

"In the alley, you called and you got me."

"And you are?"

"Not important. All you need to know is that you're lucky you're so cute, and I decided to help you."

"But not prom queen cute."

"Definitely not."

They both smiled, but Mina realized with a start that he'd never answered her question.

"So about the Grimoire," Jared continued. "It was initially a token bestowed upon the brothers by a sprite. She didn't agree with the Fae running amok in the human world – not all of us do, you know. So instead of impeding the brothers like so many other Fae, she became their ally. She stole the Story when it was new in power and split it in an attempt to limit the damage. She essentially made its doppelganger and gave it to the Grimm brothers as a guidebook. Only when you split a powerful object, the lines of good versus evil aren't separated equally, and there are always side effects."

"Let me get this straight. So you're saying that the Grimoire is like the Good Witch of the East, here on the human plane, here to help me, and guide me. While the Story is the same Wicked Witch of the West, only more powerful and evil, and essentially wants to kill me?"

"More or less, that about sums it up."

"Yikes. I really am doomed."

"I wouldn't say it wants to kill you. It wants you to complete the tales. Remember, the more you complete, the stronger it becomes. I just don't think it wants you to complete all of them."

"So how do I know how to complete the tales?"

"Some of it is based on intuition. The Grimms were always a smart bunch, or so they say. And through years of participating in the story, Grimm descendants seem to have their own kind of magic. You'll pick up on things, notice coincidences. A coincidence is often a sign that something in the Fae world is interacting on this plane."

Mina thought about showing up at the Carmichaels', and Brody running over her bike. Coincidence, or was it more likely the Fae meddling in her affairs? After a few moments, Jared got to his feet and changed the wooden sword into a small knife, and began explaining different ways to hold the knife and how to use the forearm to block downward thrusts. He ran her through some exercises and then asked her to attack him.

"I can't," Mina whined.

"Yes, you can."

"No, I don't think I can anymore. I'm cold, tired, and don't want to hurt you."

"Mina, you have to. Your life depends on it." Jared was getting angry.

"I told you, I can't."

"Do it for your brother. Do it for Charlie!" he yelled. "Do it for your father!"

That was what made Mina step back and blink in surprise. How did he know so much about her father? Was this some sort of sick joke? Mina gripped the stupid knife and felt herself go tense in preparation to attack. He was lying to her, or, as he said, manipulating the truth. He knew more than he was telling.

"What do you know about my father?" Mina yelled angrily, hot tears burning in her eyes.

"I know that he was full of himself. James didn't think he needed help and wouldn't take it when offered. He tried to face the Story on his own terms, unprepared, and paid the ultimate price for his stubbornness. And you're going to end up just like him if you don't prepare yourself," Jared called. Mina felt her body tense up like a tightly wound spring. "You're weak," Jared continued. "If you don't get stronger, you're going to doom your mother to mourning not one child, but two."

That was the final straw; Mina grabbed her wooden knife and jumped at Jared, trying to push him more than hit him.

Jared pushed her back easily until she stumbled in the sand. "Come on, you can do this. Fight me."

Mina hung her head in shame, her heart pounding frantically in her chest. She wanted to protect her family, her brother, but Jared's boot camp, encouragement had the opposite effect. She didn't want to watch her mother suffer again. Perhaps her mom was right—they should leave, and get as far away from here from possible. They should try to outrun the Story.

Mina tossed the enchanted knife as hard as she could, watching as it created spirals in the lake after it disappeared into the dark depths. She wiped her eyes with the cuff of her jacket and walked away from Jared toward the road.

"Where are you going?" he asked.

"Away, far away." Mina kept walking toward the main road. It seemed really far, and her calves were burning from walking in the sand.

"You can't escape the Story," Jared called, hoping to spur her back to fighting.

"No, I can't. But I can run."

Jogging to catch up with her, Jared tried to grab her shoulder and turn her to look at him, but she started pushing and hitting him.

"Go away. Don't touch me!" Mina was crying hard. "You've brought me nothing but pain. I hate you." She turned her face up to him in defiance, her brown eyes sparkling with tears. Jared's sculpted jaw twitched with hidden anger.

Mina flailed, but Jared grasped her wrists to keep her from hitting him. Eventually she quit struggling and stood still, quietly looking out over the water, refusing to make eye contact. When a soft tear fell on his hand, Jared let go of her as if her tear had burned his hand. As soon as he released her wrists, Mina pulled away from him and marched toward the road.

She had no plan, but at the moment she spotted a familiar green pick-up truck barreling down the road. Mina waved her arms furiously, and soon she had a bewildered Asian couple in a green truck opening the back door to let her in. She refused to look out the window at Jared as the truck sped away

CHAPTER 17

As soon as Mina got upstairs, she decided to call Brody and apologize for not meeting him after school. But there was no need, because once she reached the top landing there was a beautiful present with a large red bow on top. Mina screamed with delight, and Sara opened the door and laughed.

"It arrived a few hours ago. I couldn't wait for you to see it." Sara gently touched the bow and fingered a brown paper envelope. "There's even a card for you, Mina."

Mina ran her fingers over the handle bars of the red, fully restored vintage bike. It was the exact year as her other one, but with actual working brakes and a kickstand. She tore the red card open without even bothering to read her name on the front.

Mina,

Please forgive me for running out yesterday. I had a lot on my mind, mostly you. Ever since you risked your life to save me, I haven't been able to stop thinking about you, and I don't want to.

I want to be more than friends. I want to be the one to rush in and save you time and time again. I want to be your Prince. Please accept this gift and go with me to the Enchanted Dance.

Yours forever,
Brody Carmichael

158

P.S. Please say you will go.

P.P.S. If you don't say yes, you can still keep the bike.

P.P.P.S. Say YES!

Attached was also Brody's phone number. Mina jumped up and down in excitement and showed her mother the note. She rushed inside and grabbed the cordless phone from its hanger by the fridge. Her fingers were shaking so badly, she had to redial the number twice.

When Brody's deep voice answered the phone, Mina almost lost her nerve and found she couldn't immediately speak.

"Mina, is that you?"

"Yes, it's me." She smacked her head, wishing she could have thought of something better to have said.

"I missed you after school. Is everything okay?"

"Yes, it's fine. I'm sorry, it was, um…family business that kept me from meeting you, but don't worry. I wasn't in any danger."

"Oh!" He sounded relieved. "Is that why you called?"

Mina smiled into the phone. "I called because I love the bike. Thank you. When did you have time to find one just like it?"

Brody laughed softly into the phone, a whisper of breath that made Mina shiver in delight. "I actually ordered it the same day I rode over yours. I was going to tell you about it in the car but decided to surprise you instead. So have you decided about the dance?"

Mina couldn't keep the smile off her face. "I don't know if dancing is how I would want to spend my birthday."

"Friday is your birthday? I didn't know. We can do something else, if you want."

"No, I think spending my birthday with you would be the perfect gift." Mina smiled over the phone.

"So decide on what fairy tale couple you would like to go as, and then give me a call. I would prefer to not go as the frog prince, if you get my drift. Green and slimy doesn't look good on me."

Mina was pacing her room and thinking of some of her favorite fairy tale characters when she passed her bedroom mirror. She stared at her reflection and touched the fabric of her red jacket, a reminder of the many piles of red clothes that littered the floor. Mina realized that no matter what fairy tale princess or character she would try to go as, the Story would keep making her into the same one.

"How about Red Riding Hood?" Mina intoned sadly.

Brody's voice brightened. "Then I will be your hunter. Never fear, Mina, I'll keep the big bad wolf away."

Those words sent a tingle of dread through her limbs. She felt the power of the Story at work and actually feared that very conclusion.

***

After the phone call, Mina climbed out her window and made her way up to her rooftop retreat. It was just after dark when she pulled out the red notebook. She decided to look through the Grimoire where her mom wouldn't worry. For Sara, out of sight, out of mind, really was the best medicine. Mina reclined in the lounge chair and flipped through the notebook's pages. Still only one story. She caressed the lines and spoke to the Grimoire.

"So there's this dance and this boy. I really want to go, but I'm scared of what will happen. Do you think you can help me? I could really use all the help I can get. Please."

Mina waited as if for a response, but the wind chose that moment to pick up and swirl fallen leaves around the rooftop retreat like mini tornadoes. She dropped the notebook, and the wind blew the pages closed. Mina felt the hairline crackle of power crawl over her arms, and she knew that something was near.

"I take it that was a no," a masculine voice said behind her.

Mina turned and grabbed the Grimoire, holding it to her chest protectively, until she saw that it was Jared on the other side of the roof.

"What are you doing here?" Mina snapped.

"I'm surprised you're asking the book for help. I thought you had decided to run away. You certainly seem to be good at it." Jared walked past Mina, ignoring her to admire a rosebush growing up a brick wall.

"I know that I can't run forever, but I thought I could at least get away from you. But even that seems impossible now." Mina turned her back on Jared, and began to pick up her jacket and fold it over her arm. She didn't hear Jared move, but in one second he was next to her, grabbing her wrist, holding it up to the waning light so he could see a faint outline of bruising. He lightly rubbed the bruises with his thumbs.

Mina's eyes widened, and she jerked her hands out of his in surprise. A caress from Jared was the last thing she would have expected. His eyes turned dark, his expression unreadable. Mina found herself rubbing her own wrists, whether to rub his touch away or soothe the pain, she wasn't sure.

"You can't run anymore. It's too late." Jared turned his back on her and looked out over the roofs of the international district, his dark hair blowing slightly in the wind. "It was almost past the point of no return, once you stepped into the Babushka's Bakery. The power compelled you to enter the tale and act. It placed you in the position, and you chose. It's too late for you, Wilhelmina Grimm, great-great-great-granddaughter of Wilhelm Grimm. And you're going to need my help."

CHAPTER 18

Mina felt as if she was going to faint. "Why are you here, really?" Jared was really starting to scare her. "What part do you play in this?"

Jared looked at her, and she could have sworn that his skin glowed golden for one split second. But after she blinked her eyes, she decided it was just an illusion from the setting sun. The sun was covering both of them with a bright, warm glow.

He closed his eyes as if he was soaking up the sun and took a deep breath as if it was his first, or his last. "I am a part of this as much you are and have as much at stake, if not more." He sighed and looked at her. "Everything else has a time and a place, but it is not now, not yet."

Mina couldn't understand the change in his speech, why he was suddenly speaking in riddles. She shook her head as if to clear her thinking and remembered an earlier statement. "What tale are you referring to? The notebook only shows the bull and the stag."

Jared walked away from Mina back toward the edge of the roof. She had no choice but to chase after him if she wanted an answer.

"Hansel and Gretel."

"But wait, how?" Mina thought back through the day. "The bakery was the gingerbread house?"

Jared snorted. "Obviously."

"But there wasn't an old witch. No one was imprisoned."

"There wasn't? Are you positive? Think again—no one was held captive?" Jared's mouth turned up in challenge, and he actually looked at Mina in surprise.

"Well, no, we were all free to walk around. The boys did seem to act strange when the tour guide was talking, but..." Mina's eyes lit up with elation. "Wait, that's it. The tour guide didn't capture anyone, but she did captivate the boys' attention, and then seemed to settle for Brody in the end. He was the only one she really cared about. But she wasn't a horrible old woman, and she didn't try to put him in an oven. She wasn't going to eat any of the students like in the story, right?"

"Not exactly. There is a word for her kind in your world, I believe?"

"I don't understand." She turned and picked up a large rock, and held it in her hands.

"An older woman who preys on the attention of younger men. Who uses them, eats them up, and spits them out. Sound familiar?"

"A cougar?" Mina asked in disbelief.

Jared snorted again. "A man-eater."

"OH!" Mina replied, still dumbfounded. She thought back on the young Claire with her red heels and brightly painted nails, the way she sashayed when she walked and thrived on the younger male attention. It made sense.

"Your teacher was lax in his duties to watch after you and you entered the factory alone, the same as the incompetent father in the tale. Then you were greeted by the hungry female man-eater, who lured boys into her clutches with her good looks. She's quite a bit older than she looks, by the way."

"What, thirty?"

"Older."

"Forty?"

"Try one hundred and twenty."

"How is that possible? I mean, I saw her, and she didn't look a day over thirty!"

"It's the power of the tale. This particular fairy tale was set in motion a hundred years ago, in preparation for you." Jared turned and stepped closer to Mina. "Think back—didn't she seem familiar?"

"She did seem familiar, but where have I seen her before? I wouldn't know anyone one hundred and twenty years old."

"Come on, Mina. You have to figure this out for yourself. I can't solve all of the tales for you. Think hard."

Mina tried. A picture of a smiling Claire flashed into her mind, and then Claire's face after the accident seared itself into her brain. She was no longer smiling, but somber, and then Mina knew where she had seen the woman before. "Mrs. Brimwell, the wife of Larry Brimwell, the founder of the company." Mina remembered the unsmiling blonde woman from the mural.

"Very good. Anyone else?" Jared smiled encouragingly.

"Well, B.J. looks like the young boy, but there are some slight differences."

"That's because he's not the boy from the mural. He is Brimwell Jr. He is, in fact, Claire's great-grandson, although he doesn't know it."

"How can that be possible? How come the boy aged but Claire didn't?"

"Because the tale didn't need both of them to live forever, just one. The makings for the Hansel and Gretel tale were all there, so fate used what it had. It helps that Claire is part Fae and won't age as long as she continues to bring boys and girls through the factory. The power of the tale keeps her young.

She literally feeds off the energy of the youth, especially boys. I told you earlier that Fae feed off human energy and feelings."

"But what happens now?"

"Well, you saved Hansel from being fed to the man-eater by interrupting the tour. Brimwell Jr. won't allow any more tours for fear of a lawsuit. You, Mina, outsmarted the story's old woman, or witch, and completed the tale."

"But doesn't the story end with the old woman getting pushed into the oven and burned alive?" Mina shivered at the thought. "I can't do that."

"Doesn't have to. As long as you fulfill certain requirements of the tales, the Story will be satisfied. The heroine saved the boy and defeated the witch. The power of that tale has ended. Now the enchantment that kept Claire young will fade away, and she will age and die. When she dies, the tale will be complete."

"Oh." Mina was saddened. Her actions would now cause Claire to die.

"Relax, Mina, she had lived a very long and youthful life. It's time for her to join her son and husband."

"I feel horrible, like I've done something wrong." Mina clutched her stomach and sat down on the edge of the roof. It was worse than she imagined. She didn't have the stomach to do the task put before her.

"So do you see why you can't run anymore, Mina? Your mother can no longer protect you. You've already completed two of the Grimm tales. Hansel and Gretel and another, lesser tale when you found the Grimoire."

"The Bull and the Stag," Mina murmured. "But that didn't involve anyone dying." She shook her head. "Jared, I think I feel sick. You should leave."

Jared reached down and helped her back up. He kept one hand on her arm and led her to the fire escape steps.

By the time she'd maneuvered the steps to her window, Mina was so exhausted she didn't even confront Jared on how he knew where she lived. She had begun to accept that there were numerous things about Jared she would never understand, and she was too tired to care.

She stepped off the last stair and was about to crawl through the window when she felt her knees go weak. Jared reached out to steady her. Mina's legs were numb, and as she moved away, pinpricks of blood rushed through her lower limbs.

Jared called out to Mina when she'd safely made it over the sill. "You should keep the Grimoire close to you at all times."

She bobbed her head in answer, never once looking him in the eyes.

"Be careful. I don't know if you realize it, but you're already in another fairy tale."

Mina's head snapped up to look at him, eyes wide. "What? Is it that obvious?"

Jared shook his head and muttered the word "hopeless" under his breath. He pointed to her jackets. "There is a reason you can't go out of the house without wearing red hoods and you keep meeting up with Grey Tail."

Mina let out a puff of air she didn't know she was holding. "I know, Red Riding Hood."

"I suspect your clothes will return to normal after you complete this tale. That is, if you live through your final encounter with the wolf."

Jared was serious. He was trying to warn her, protect her, and prepare her. She was nearly ready to ask for forgiveness and for his help once more when he shot off one final parting comment that made her blood run cold.

"I do think you need to be careful. Your rooftop isn't the safest place to cry yourself to sleep."

Mina jumped away in alarm. She slammed the window and pulled the shade closed in frustration. She could hear Jared laughing from the other side of the glass. When her heart calmed down and she got her hands to quit shaking, she opened the window again, and he was gone.

CHAPTER 19

The next day flew by. There were no strange storybook appearances by animals, unexplained happenings, or surprise attacks by wolves. Mina felt she knew why. With the date of the dance set, she could almost feel the power building, preparing for the final chapter. She read what she could of Red Riding Hood but was too scared to touch the Grimoire. Instead, she kept the Grimoire in her backpack at all times. Every time her fingers grazed the notebook, it seemed to hum with excitement, especially the closer it came to the dance. The more it hummed, the more nervous Mina became, until she began hiding the book and locking it in a drawer in her room.

Jared barely acknowledged Mina at school but seemed to always be hovering just on the outskirts, watching, waiting. He hardly spoke except when spoken to, and his sudden change in countenance scared off the rest of the students.

Brody soon noticed Jared's motorcycle following them in his rearview mirror day after day, which lead to an altercation after school. Brody and Mina were on the way to his car, but when they crossed the parking lot, he passed his own vehicle and walked over to a familiar black motorcycle. Mina saw the set of his jaw and knew immediately what was going to happen. She, too, had seen Jared following them everywhere they went.

"Brody, don't. Let's just go."

"Not until I speak to Jared."

"It's not worth it."

"You and your safety are definitely worth it. I'm not leaving until I've spoken my mind."

He didn't have to wait long before Jared turned the corner, stopping in his tracks when he saw them. "That's my bike you're leaning on," Jared said carefully. "You scratch it, you buy it."

"Maybe I should, and then you couldn't stalk Mina anymore."

"Get real, I'm not stalking her. I'll leave that to you, lover boy."

"Uh-uh. I've seen you. After school, before school, following her on *this* bike."

"Guys, can we please drop this," Mina tried, but neither boy even looked at her.

"I haven't been following you anywhere," Jared said. "Are you sure it was this bike?"

Brody blinked in thought, "I could have sworn it was you. Black bike and helmet?"

"No, I swear to you. Not me. Must be some crazy *fan* of yours," Jared answered lightly, but to Mina he looked distinctly worried, and she felt an awful pit begin to form in the hollow of her stomach. Who had been following her?

"And what about at school?" Brody continued. Mina's cheeks turned red as she realized a crowd had begun to form. "You can't deny that you're always watching her. I've seen you, and you're making her uncomfortable."

Mina held her breath as Jared's eyes flickered between them, the longest pause in the history of long pauses.

"I was trying to find an opportunity to ask her to the dance. That's all." He winked at Mina, likely a nod to his clever excuse, but one that Brody would almost certainly take the wrong way.

"Too late. She's going with me. So find someone else to torment."

Mina didn't have time to react or yell a warning before Brody's fist connected with Jared's jaw, knocking him backward over the bike. Mina cringed as the bike and Jared crashed to the cement in a pile of metal and bones.

Brody stood over the fallen Jared, rubbing his fist. "That's for creeping Mina out. I don't care what you say. I still think it was you following her!" Brody pulled out a wad of cash and threw it on Jared's chest. "And that's for scratching your bike." He stormed across the parking lot toward his car.

With tears in her eyes, Mina reached down to help Jared up, but he waved her off. He picked up his bike in one fluid motion, ignoring the cash that was blowing away in the wind as he inspected the damage. Some of the students began to run after the bills as they tumbled away.

"I'm so sorry. Jared, I had no idea that he was going to—"

"No," Jared interrupted. "Don't apologize for him. He's a big boy. And truthfully, I think I like him better now." Making sure no one was looking, Jared rubbed his hands over the dents, and with a glow of power they began to fill themselves back out. The scratches glowed and began to spiral out, erasing themselves and leaving no trace of damage. "But, Mina, you know that wasn't me following you, right? I wasn't lying about that."

A roar of a motorcycle engine coming to life made Jared's and Mina's heads snap up in the direction of the street. A man dressed in all black was sitting on a motorcycle, watching them.

Mina felt a trickle of cold sweat slide down her back.

"I recognize the scent," Jared said quietly. "Grey Tail." They watched as the black reflective helmet nodded at Jared before tearing off down the road, leaving a trail of burned rubber behind him.

"What's going on, Jared?" Mina asked in as brave a voice as she could muster.

"Time is running short. The pack is gathering."

***

Two weeks before the dance, Mina noticed that Jared had made himself scarce. He didn't attend classes the rest of the week. She knew he, too, could feel what was coming. When Mina did see him, he always seemed to be walking a fine line between barely controlling his anger and being completely aloof. He avoided Brody entirely.

Surprisingly, he appeared Thursday during lunch. He walked directly toward her and slid onto the bench next to Mina, ignoring her presence as he asked her best friend, Nan Taylor, to the dance.

Mina waited for him to look at her, to glance her way, acknowledge her with a self-satisfied smirk or even a frown. She needed confirmation from Jared that she wasn't in this alone, that he had her back or was there to help her out. She waited for Jared to bait her with a snide comment or joke. He didn't.

When Nan accepted his offer, Jared squeezed her hand and told her he would call her. He exited the table as silently as he had appeared, without a backward glance at Mina.

Mina was crushed. Without Jared's help, Mina knew she couldn't finish the tale. Only Brody's weight on the bench snapped Mina out of her depression.

"What's going on?" he asked Nan.

Nan positively glowed with excitement when she told Brody about her date. Brody's smile turned into a frown as Nan spent the rest of her lunch hour talking about costumes.

CHAPTER 20

When Mina told her mother about the dance theme, Sara wisely didn't say anything, but gave her daughter a wary look. She even helped pick out Mina's costume. The costume shop was dimly lit, and smelled like a cross between shoe polish and a school locker room.

"It smells like old people," Mina whispered to her mom, wrinkling her nose in distaste.

Sara tried not to laugh. "It's the moth balls, honey. There are a lot of old clothes here. They are vintage, after all."

Mina did her best to put on a smile. To Sara, "vintage" meant cheaper than the mall and one step up from a thrift store. Mina tried to look enthusiastic when the sales lady greeted them. She only hoped the dresses didn't smell like the store.

Just for fun, Mina tried on various renaissance gowns and princess costumes, probably castoffs from some long-ago school plays. But every costume had the same problem: It didn't fit with what the Story wanted. It seemed as if the Story was controlling even Mina's dance attire. Every dress had a fault or wouldn't fit.

"This would be a great Cinderella gown." Sara grunted as she pulled and fumbled with the zipper. "It must be caught on something." Sara tried and tried but could not get the zipper to cooperate. Even when Mina explained that the Story wouldn't let her go as any other character, Sara seemed determined to try to change the Story's mind.

"Try this one instead." Sara held up a sapphire-blue dress with long, delicate sleeves. "You could be Sleeping Beauty. That tale doesn't have any wolves." She smiled hopefully, but Mina detected the stress that was ticking under her mother's left eye. When that dress, too, refused to zip, Sara was awash in tears of frustration. A store seamstress, Molly, came over and tried to help, but neither one could get the zipper to work.

"That is so strange," the seamstress commented wryly. She fumbled with the zipper and could find no cloth or string hindering the teeth. She tried a different dress and tested the zipper before asking Mina to step into it. "Let's try a larger dress."

Mina rolled her eyes and stepped into the next size up, blowing her bangs out of her eyes. She was exhausted from trying on dresses. Yes, she would have absolutely loved the blue Cinderella gown, but she knew better than to get her hopes up.

"It's stuck!" Molly gasped out. She tugged and tugged on the zipper, which had worked perfectly only minutes ago. "I don't know what to tell you. I was sure it would work." She was flustered and didn't know how to appease Sara, who was by now moved to tears of frustration.

"Oh, my poor girl!" Sara cried and blew her nose on a tissue from her purse. She knew what the signs meant as well as Mina.

Mina usually enjoyed dress shopping, the few times they had the money to do so, but this was getting ridiculous. Mina scanned the rack of dresses, and her eye stopped on a deep red one.

"That one." Mina pointed to the rack, and Molly jumped up and pushed the dresses to the side. She pulled out a beautiful red dress that flowed out in billows from the petite corseted waist. Most of the fabric was gathered and pleated down the back in a late Victorian style. The corset was a deep red, made from many different fabrics that sparkled and twinkled with the lights.

The dress was gorgeous—at least the Story had good taste. This was the one she would have chosen, if it hadn't been red.

"I don't think I've ever seen this one," the seamstress exclaimed, gushing over the dress, then taking one looked at Mina's petite figure and announcing, "I'm afraid it might be too small."

"It will fit." Mina knew deep down it would. This was the dress she was supposed to wear.

Sara helped Mina into the dress, her hands shaking as she went to try the zipper. "I can't." Sara backed away from the dress to sit on a small pink padded stool by the mirror. She held her hand to her mouth fearfully.

Molly stepped forward and pulled the zipper up with ease, carefully hooking the top eyelet.

"Well, I'll be. I would have thought it was two sizes too small, but it fits like it was made for you."

Mina's eyes went wide when she saw her reflection. Molly began cinching the back of the corset and tugging the ribbons and arraying them. Mina had to actually pinch herself to make sure she wasn't dreaming.

She looked different: older, more mature, and beautiful. She couldn't remember ever looking this stunning in her whole life. Her dark brown hair flowed down her back and was lost among the ribbons of the corset. Her eyes looked huge, and her lips red and full. Her nose, the one she always feared was too small for her face, looked straight and perfect. She gave a sleeve a cursory sniff and sighed in relief when it smelled of cinnamon and honey instead of mothballs.

Molly stood back to admire Mina. "Wow. You look like something out of a fairy tale."

Sara cried harder.

Mina spun around and looked at the dress from every angle in the multiple mirrors. It was better than any princess dress she had tried on so far. Mina's only worry was that the dress had layers and layers of material in the back. It would make it very difficult to run in, if it came down to it.

"We'll take it," Mina told the girl, not even bothering to ask the price was. If the Story wanted her to wear the dress, then the Story had better provide.

Unsurprising to Mina, Molly had to check the price on the tag twice, confirming the price. "I can't believe it. I didn't even know we had dresses for this price, but I've checked with the manager, and she thinks it's fine. It seems you have yourself a dress." She clapped and pressed her hands together in excitement.

Mina was about to get down off the platform when Molly held up something hidden by the folds of Mina's dress. "Oh, look, it comes with a cape and hood."

Of course it would, Mina thought dryly.

CHAPTER 21

Mina couldn't stop pacing in the small carpeted living room, waiting for Brody to pick her up. Even Charlie sat in the window seat, nose pressed firmly to the glass, fogging it up with every breath he took. Mina wondered who was more excited.

Sara had been unusually quiet and had become more withdrawn as the time of the dance drew near. She did her motherly duty and helped her daughter do her hair. She made all the appropriate comments and oohed and aahed at all the right times. But nothing could get her excited about this evening, knowing the tale was heading toward its climax.

This was one of the tales that had secretly haunted Sara as a child. When her grandmother read her the story as a child, she'd wake up with nightmares about a wolf attacking her in her bed. And now here she was, sixteen years later on the day of her daughter's birthday, her greatest fear finally coming to life.

The morning had started out peacefully enough. Sara had made Mina a two-tiered white frosted birthday cake with light pink flowers and strawberry cream cheese filling. She invited Nan Taylor and the Wongs, who had decorated a section of their restaurant with bright pink and blue streamers that Mina suspected might have been left over from a baby shower.

The Wongs sang "Happy Birthday" off key, while Nan and Charlie made faces during the whole song. Nan went so far as to even add "you look like a monkey and smell like one, too," just so Charlie would giggle.

The Wongs gave Mina her birthday gift in a Chinese takeout box, which included a gift card to the mall. Nan's gift was a new pair of cute black flats, which she promptly asked to borrow next week, after Mina had worn them. Charlie gave her a new stationery set and journal, which was a very thoughtful gift for a boy.

Mina was surprised when the restaurant door opened and Brody walked in. She'd thought he would wait to give her his present later that evening, and was totally unprepared for his arrival. Mina's hand went to her sloppy ponytail in distress, then remembered she was still wearing her pajama bottoms and an ugly, over-large red sweatshirt.

But one look at her, and Brody was all smiles. He, naturally, looked as handsome as ever in a white button-up shirt, dark distressed jeans—probably his family's own label— and black shoes. His blond hair touched the collar of his shirt in the back, and it looked like he hadn't shaved in a few days. But the whole look was very pleasing to the eye. Mina immediately stepped behind Nan to hide her pajama shorts.

"Hey," Mina called out, embarrassed.

"Hey, you." Brody smiled at her awkwardness, and Mina immediately felt like an idiot. She knew that Brody didn't care what she wore.

She stepped closer and whispered, "What are you doing here? I didn't think you were coming until tonight."

"Well, I heard a rumor that you were having a birthday party, and yet I didn't get the invite. I thought I might come and crash it." Brody looked past Mina to acknowledge Nan with a slight nod of his head.

Mina spun to look at her best friend. "Oh, I see. Let me clarify. I bet a little birdy *tweeted* you the exact time and location. What a smart little bird."

Nan whistled and suddenly found one of the red and gold paper lanterns in the restaurant particularly interesting.

When Mina turned around, Brody pecked her on the cheek and handed her a beautifully wrapped present, wrapped in pristine white paper and accented with a simple red velvet ribbon on top. Mina's smiled coyly at Brody and pulled the ribbon to reveal a brand-new candy-apple red LG phone.

"What? Brody, we can't afford this." Mina panicked and looked at her mother in surprise. Cell phone plans alone tended to be expensive, especially for such a nice phone as this. "Brody, thank you, but I can't accept it." She handed the box back to Brody, who held up his hands and backed away.

"Can't return it. Besides, it's been added to our plan. With how many phones we have, it wasn't anything for our family to add one more."

If he said it to make Mina feel less guilty, it only had the opposite effect. Mina looked toward her mother for help.

Sara stepped forward. "Brody, it's a wonderful gift, but I don't know if I feel comfortable with your family paying for a cell phone for my daughter. Maybe next year we can afford one, but not right now."

"I understand, Sara. And I wouldn't normally offer this kind of gift, but I felt you would understand the necessity of Mina being able to call us in case of an emergency. If she were ever in trouble or needed help, she would need a cell phone to call for help. For my own peace of mind, and so I can sleep at night, I hope you'll let her keep the gift." Sara was about to counter again, but Brody was too quick. "And by next year if you want to take over the plan, we can arrange it."

Sara seemed relieved and nodded her head in agreement.

Mina felt a hint of panic and turned to Brody, worry etched in her face. "But what if we should...or you decide that you no longer..." Mina couldn't even speak it. What if they broke up? Would he take the phone away?

"It doesn't matter—my offer still stands. Besides, I've already programmed my number, your mother's, and the fire department. I think you're covered." He took the red phone out of the box and handed it to Mina.

The phone felt light and delicate, and Mina knew she was destined to drop it and break it into a thousand little pieces. How could she possibly not lose the device, unless it was stapled to her forehead?

"Well, you seem to have missed one VERY important number." Nan stepped forward and took the phone from Mina. "What?" she exclaimed, scrolling through the contacts. "You programmed your number as two. TWO! That definitely has to change. After the emergency department, the next number should definitely be her BEST FRIEND." Nan held the phone away from Brody as he tried to snatch it back from her. They began to argue over who should be number two on speed dial.

"Too late, mine's already there. You'll have to take four." Brody chuckled.

"As if! You take four. You've only known Mina a few weeks. I've been her best friend for two years. See...two. I should be two," Nan continued.

Mina looked at her mom and saw a slight grin. Maybe, just maybe, everything would turn out all right.

Brody left shortly after he challenged Nan to Paper, Rock, Scissors, and won, for the right to be number two on her speed dial. After winning, he conceded to give Nan and Jared a ride to the dance as well, as a consolation prize. Brody gave Mina a small peck on the lips, whispered "happy birthday," and told her he would see her soon.

That was eight hours ago.

Now Mina had only been wearing heels for an hour, and was already eager to kick them off and scandalize the school with her bare feet. She could never understand women's obsession with high heels. Sure, they made make you look taller and slimmer, but was it worth it to have to limp around the whole night from blisters? Mina didn't think so.

Just as she was about to find a pair of flip flops in her closet, Charlie started waving and knocking on the glass. Mina looked down into the street and was surprised to see a stretch SUV limo appear, with a familiar blonde head poking through the sun roof. Nan was waving like a maniac, and a minute later the dark head of Jared appeared next to her, looking somber as ever.

From the angle of the window, Mina saw a limo door open and close, and knew that Brody was on his way up the stairs.

"Mom! How do I look?" Mina called out, hoping to fix any last-minute curls that had come loose from their bobby pins.

"You look beautiful." Sara came over and gave her daughter a kiss on her cheek. "Please, Mina, be careful tonight."

"I will." Mina knew her mother was worried. She wasn't the only one. Tonight she was more grateful than ever that the Grimoire was so slim, as she was able to tuck it between her body and the corset, cinched tightly and within easy grasp. She had whispered and coaxed the book into an even smaller, slimmer form to fit in her bodice.

A knock came at the door, and Charlie ran to open it. His mouth dropped in shock, and he backed away, pulling the door open so Brody could step through. Mina froze mid-step as his tall form entered the kitchen. Brody looked deadly. He hadn't taken any shortcuts in designing his costume, and now wore leather bracers, a leather vest, and brown pants tucked into tall leather boots. Strapped to his chest she saw a belt of knives, and on his back, an actual bow and arrow. Brody was literally armed to the teeth. And incredibly hot.

Brody stumbled when he caught sight of Mina in her red dress. She felt herself blushing, but he quickly composed himself, and reached for her hand so he could bring it softly to his lips.

"Are they real?" Mina asked, reaching out to touch the daggers in the bandolier. She was a little disappointed when they bent easily.

"No, unfortunately not. I wouldn't be able to get real ones past security." He chuckled.

Mina felt another familiar tingling sensation spread throughout her body, reminding her that tonight would have a storybook ending, one way or another. The Story was already at work.

When Brody and Mina were on the landing and had shut the door, he stopped her from walking down the stairs.

"Why did you stop?" Mina was holding onto Brody's arm, her other hand gripping layers of her dress so she wouldn't trip going down the stairs.

"I wanted a moment with you alone."

"Is something wrong?" she asked. She worried that he knew something was coming as much as she did.

Brody reached up and caressed her face. "No, nothing's wrong. Everything is perfect. But with the way Nan talks, this may be our only quiet moment for the rest of the night. Even if we have to suffer Jared's presence."

Mina was once again surprised by how often Brody seemed to read her mind. She had been nervous about being in the back of a limo alone with Brody, given their new relationship status. More than anything, she was nervous that she would somehow resort back to the awkward stage of their friendship, and not be able to remain calm, cool, and collected.

"No, that's fine. I'm happy that you invited Nan." Mina's shoulders slumped at the thought of facing Jared and being shunned.

"But not Jared?" Brody could read the strain in her voice.

"No, I'm glad. Really I am."

"He was part of the deal. I knew you would want to have Nan close to you, and he was just the carry-on luggage. If he makes you uncomfortable, just let me know." Brody rubbed his finger along Mina's jaw and leaned down to kiss her sweetly on the mouth. Mina reached up and drew him closer. He tasted of richness and warmth. Brody wrapped his arms around her, and Mina felt safe and secure—until a loud horn blared from downstairs.

Mina pulled back from the kiss and grinned. "That would be Nan. Her timing is usually pretty terrible."

Brody helped Mina down the stairs and opened the door onto the street. As soon as she popped out the door, Nan jumped down out of the driver's seat and over to Mina. "Oh, my goodness, you look beautiful. I never imagined red looking that good on you, but wow!"

Nan's own hair had been piled high and sprayed with white, with white ringlets falling down the back of her neck and around her face. She had a flowing white dress and red, red lips; she was obviously the Snow Queen.

"And wait till you see Jared," she told Mina. "Is he hot, or what?"

Just then Jared stepped out of the limo, and Mina clutched onto Brody's arm. Jared hadn't dressed as a specific character, but the costume seemed so fitting it was hard to remember what he looked like in anything else. His thin frame was the perfect complement to the white Victorian shirt with the tie-up collar and silver doublet with dark black pants. His skin glowed in the darkness, accented by his dark hair,, though that may have been a trick of the light from the neon store fronts across the street. His stormy eyes shone like molten silver.

"You clean up nice," Mina said, trying to ease the tension in the air. "This is a good look for you."

"Thanks," he muttered. "You look…fantastic."

Mina smirked. "Why, Jared, that may be the nicest thing you've ever said to me."

"I cannot tell a lie," he replied, shrugging before helping Nan into the car. It came off as a joke, but only Mina knew the truth behind those words.

Brody led her slowly to the back of the limo, Mina walking on the balls of her feet so as not to damage her heels in the grass. He opened the door to let her slide in. Mina was so short she had a bit of trouble maneuvering up into the limo, especially with the dress. Once she was in, Nan slid in behind her and moved down toward the drink bar. "Look, sparkling cider." She opened the cider and poured a few glasses.

Mina took the glass and sipped it cautiously, fully aware of Jared's direct gaze. Nan handed a drink to Brody, who put it in a cup holder. As they took off, Nan fiddled with the radio stations and finally found a rock station worth jamming to.

The music seemed a surreal backdrop to the scene in the limo: Nan bobbing her head to the music; Jared sitting against the black leather, brooding silently across from her; and Brody decked out in knives, his bow and arrow parked beside him, studying everyone with an intense look.

"Happy birthday, MINA!" Nan yelled out and giggled. Jared's head flipped to Mina with a look of horror on his face. She supposed she hadn't told him that the day she would face one of the scariest tales would also be her birthday. Not that he'd asked. Mina broke eye contact first and nervously played with a pleat on her skirt.

Her head started to pound from the loud music, and she desperately wished the limo would fly to the school so they could already be there. The limo ride, though beautiful, was unbearably tense. She sighed in relief when the driver turned into the school parking lot and pulled up to drop them off at the entrance. Then she saw the crowd. More than two dozen students were milling around outside, and several started whistling when they saw the stretch limo, knowing only Brody Carmichael could be inside. Among them were Savannah White and all her friends.

When Mina and Nan stepped out of the limo behind the two hottest boys in school, Savannah's smile turned downright ugly. She'd come dressed in light blue, her blonde hair piled high in a bun with a tiara. She was obviously Cinderella, and Priscilla, with her green dress and stuffed frog purse, the princess from "The Princess and the Frog."

Mina tried not to look Savannah's way, but she could see her whispering furiously to Pri out of the corner of her eye. She felt sorry for her, for a moment, knowing Brody had once meant something to her, too. But then she heard her snicker

"Little Grimy Hood" as she passed by, and felt all sympathy drain from her mind.

When they arrived at the doors, the security guards did indeed do a pat-down and checked all of Brody's fake knives and arrows. Mina considered asking Jared to make her a weapon later in the night.

Nan and Mina entered the gym, and gasped in surprise at the visual wonderland the student council had created, complete with sparkling lights and full-sized set pieces. Rapunzel's tower had been set up next to the giant gingerbread house and wishing well. Even the bench where Mina and Brody had shared their first kiss now looked as romantic as a fairy tale. Giant gates and an archway sectioned off the areas for pictures, food, and dancing.

Fog machines were hidden around the gym, forming misty paths, the colored lights creating ambiance. Even the D.J. who was spinning had gotten into the enchanted theme, donning ogre ears and large patchwork clothes.

Dancing on the floor was a visual montage of fairy tale, storybook, and mythical animals. A minotaur was trying to pour punch for a unicorn. A fawn was dancing with a goose girl maiden. Mina saw various wolves, sheep, and dragons, usually milling about in clusters off the dance floor. Those who weren't animals had chosen to be a prince, princess, or knight. Frank and Steve could be seen pretending to joust, using stick horses and the school's flags.

D.J. Ogre, his requested moniker for the night, pulled out some slower music, and the dance floor that was hopping began to empty as couples filed on.

"Do you want to dance?" Brody asked.

"I'm not sure you should risk it," Mina said, flushing bright red.

"It'll be fine, if you let me lead." Brody took Mina's hands and led her onto the floor. He was right; as long as Mina let Brody lead, she didn't have any problems finding the rhythm or staying away from his feet. It was perhaps the most graceful she'd felt all her life. Of course, the dress didn't hurt.

"See, you're doing great," Brody said, encouraging Mina and holding her closer. "You know, I should have thought twice about bringing you here."

Mina was startled by his words. Was he now realizing that he was ashamed of her? Had she stepped on his toes? She'd thought that she was doing just fine. "What do you mean?"

"I thought that I could handle bringing you to the dance, but I'm finding that's not true." His hands tightened around her waist, and he leaned in to whisper in her ear. "Every Steve, Frank, and Larry can't take their eyes off you." Brody nodded with his chin toward a crowd of boys, and Mina sneaked a quick peek over her shoulder before turning bright pink with embarrassment. He was right—everyone was staring at them.

"Maybe it's you. You do usually have a lot of people staring at you," she tried.

"That's kind, but I doubt that many boys at our school find me so attractive." As they circled the room, Brody glared at the boys, and a few actually turned away in embarrassment. Some began texting on their phones, while others refused to budge their gaze.

"I'm sorry. I hope I did nothing to embarrass you."

"Don't apologize. This is not your fault. You can't help looking so gorgeous."

Mina's cheeks turned pink. When the song began to die down, Brody had finally had enough. "Will you be safe next to Nan? I really want to go talk to those guys." Brody walked

Mina over to Nan, who was talking animatedly to a short boy with glasses.

Once Brody walked away, Nan leaned over and whispered to her, "Can you believe the attention you're getting? I've never seen anything like it." She nudged Mina and pointed to another group of guys wearing various animal masks.

"Nan, I don't think they attend our school," Mina whispered. She was right; there was a completely different group of students who couldn't or wouldn't take their eyes off her. To test a theory, Mina looped her arm through Nan's and walked over to a food table. They followed at a distance, trying to not draw attention.

"They ARE following you!" Nan mouthed.

"Where's Brody?" Mina walked back to where she had last seen him, but he was gone. "I have to find Jared!" Mina called out, feeling herself panic. If she couldn't have Brody by her side, at least she wanted to know where Jared was.

"I don't know. He danced with me for a few songs, but then he disappeared. Mina, those guys are coming over her.'"" Nan nodded with her chin to the group of guys again. They had stopped trying to blend in with the crowd and now moved menacingly toward Mina and Nan.

The tingling sensation began in Mina's body, and she knew it was time. But instead of rising to the occasion, she lost her nerve. "Nan, I have to get out of here." She began to pull on Nan's arm, and together they turned and headed for an exit.

The first door was blocked by Rapunzel's tower, and the second was right between the group of unknown guys. No way was she heading there.

"The stage. There's another exit behind the D.J. on the stage," Nan yelled over the music. They ducked under a column of streamers and balloons, and headed up the steps to the stage. Once onstage, Mina looked out over the dance floor and saw two groups of people making their way toward the stage. Who were they? What did they want? When they passed through the foggy dance floor and the lasers hit them, Mina noticed a slight blurring of their human forms. What she saw for that split second chilled her to the bone. One of them looked up to the stage and saw Mina's terrified face. He ditched the mask and practically drooled with pleasure at seeing her so scared.

"Here!" Nan shouted, having pulled a curtain aside and found the exit door that led backstage. They ran toward the stairs that led down to the side doors, but were blocked by a large man.

"Eeep!" Nan squealed as someone grabbed her from behind and clamped a fist over her mouth.

Another figure loomed out of the dark. Mina screamed in fright, but it couldn't be heard over the thumping of the bass.

"Ah, Little Red, Little Red, you strayed from the path." The one Jared had called Grey Tail moved in quickly. Mina tried to run, but he lunged for her and slammed her against the wall, spinning her so that her head crashed into the brick. Spots flecked across Mina's vision.

Grey Tail leaned forward and pressed his face into her neck, inhaling her scent. He brushed his teeth against a vein in her throat, following the pulse from her clavicle to chin. "Where's the book?" he whispered, growling into her ear.

"I told you before, I don't have it," Mina whimpered. The way he was leaning on her, she feared he might feel it in her bodice.

"She's lying," a woman said, her gravelly voice echoing out of the darkness.

"Does it look like I have a book on me?" Mina shouted at the figure in the dark. Her vision was swimming, and she heard a slow *click, click* in her head.

"She may have left it at home," Grey Tail said hesitantly to the dark figure, while still pressing himself close to his prey.

"You searched her home once and didn't find it. What makes you think she would have left it there now? Use your brain, you worthless dog."

Mina's vision began to clear, and she could make out the wood flooring of the stage. The clicking sound drew nearer, and slowly a pair of red high-heeled shoes came into view. She knew those heels and was about to comment on them when a hand grabbed Mina's hair roughly, digging the bobby pins deeply into her scalp and forcing her to look at the speaker.

It was Claire.

CHAPTER 22

Or what used to be Claire. She had aged considerably within a few weeks. She no longer looked to be in her thirties but now her eighties. Her hair had turned gray, and her skin was wrinkled and covered in sun spots. She had lost weight, too much of it, till there was barely a trace of the beautiful woman Mina had met once before

"This is your fault," she spat at Mina, gripping Mina's head and slamming it against the wall again, proving that her body had aged but her strength had not diminished. "I was perfect, timeless, until you showed up at my bakery. Who would have thought that an actual Grimm would walk through my doors? I'm honored, really, to be included in the infamous tales, and maybe if I had fed on an earlier school tour, I would have noticed you. Believe me, if I had, you wouldn't have survived long."

Mina shrank away from Claire's touch. Jared had said that she would eventually age and die, but Mina had thought it would take years, not days. It made her wonder even more at the depth and power of the tales.

"I'm sorry—I had no idea about the power of the tale until days later. You have to believe me."

Claire studied Mina closely. "I believe you, sweet child. But you see, we still have a problem. I don't want to age. I want to stay young forever. I want it to go back to the way it was before you showed up at my bakery."

"I can't. I don't know how to reverse what was done." Mina trembled with fear. The men who surrounded Claire stepped forward, flexing their fingers, eager for the violence to begin.

"Nonsense, you can. I've been told you're the chosen one, and you have the Grimoire. You have the power to change the tale."

"I don't," Mina cried out.

"You do!" Claire grinned evilly. "And all I think you need is some proper motivation. Bring them in, Lonetree."

Mina didn't know what to expect and was surprised when a red-haired boy she'd never seen before dragged in a compliant Savannah and Pri. They looked somewhat dazed and confused, but unharmed. The girls sat at Claire's feet, immobile, as if under a spell.

"Let them go!" Mina struggled against Grey Tail, but he grinned and squeezed Mina's arms tighter until they felt like they were about to break.

"I loved my husband," Claire said softly. "Do you know what it's like to outlive a loved one? Do you?" She screamed the last question.

"Yes," she cried. "I do. And I'm sorry."

"NO, YOU DON'T!" Claire's face froze for a moment, and then she started to laugh maniacally. "I used to feel cheated that they didn't inherit my longevity. But then I realized I was meant for much greater things. Like stopping the likes of you."

A beeping noise interrupted Claire's rant. She pulled a cell phone out of her purse and answered in a language Mina had never once heard. Even from a cruel old woman like Claire, her voice sounded breathy, melodic and mesmerizing. Mina could barely hear the voice on the other end, gruff and clipped. With a sharp click, Claire hung up the phone and studied the girls in front of her and Mina.

"Tell you what, Mina. I will let you choose who lives and who dies. I only need two of you and the Grimoire. You can't say that I'm completely heartless. I'm giving you a chance to save your own skinny neck."

Mina stared at Savannah and Pri's unresponsive bodies, and contemplated what Claire was saying. The two shallow girls seemed completely unaware of their surroundings, staring ahead blankly. Pri might have even let loose a little drool. If Mina named her enemies, she could turn over the Grimoire and still live. But she could never be that manipulative, or that heartless. This was her battle, and she knew she couldn't complete the tale only halfway. There had to be an ending.

Mina had to think quickly. Maybe Claire thought they were still trapped in the Hansel and Gretel retelling. She didn't know that the Story had moved on and lost interest in her. If Claire didn't know that Mina was now rewriting Red Riding Hood, then that could be to her advantage. But she was going to need help. Looking to her left, Mina caught Nan's angry glare. She only hoped Jared would come in time.

"Sorry, Nan, but I choose us. Let Savannah and Pri go. Nan and I will go with you, but not here. We need to know that the rest of the students will be unharmed." Nan whimpered, but Mina tried to relay through her eyes that everything would be okay.

A cackling laugh erupted from Claire's cracked lips. "You fool. I knew you would choose to save your friends. You Grimms are so predictable." Claire walked forward and through – literally through—Savannah and Pri, who disappeared into thin puffs of smoke. Illusions, the girls were illusions. Simply one of Claire's Fae tricks.

Claire roughly gripped Mina's chin and pulled the stage curtain to the side so she could see the real Savannah and Pri on the dance floor, arms waving above their heads, carefree and obviously alive.

"You made your deal, and so you'll come with us. It's easier when you don't fight it. But I'm warning you, any tricks, and it won't be the students who are harmed. It will be your mother and brother." She turned to Lonetree and Grey Tail. "Take them both—we need to leave. Now! I can feel something. Something is coming, and I don't like it."

Snapping jaws answered Claire, doubly grotesque as the wolves were still in their human form. Mina had only a moment to struggle before she was lifted into the air and then hauled over Lonetree's shoulder, which smelled of nicotine and sweat. Mina tried to scream, but his shoulder dug deeply into her stomach, cutting off her breath.

Nan fought harder and spouted incessant derogative remarks at her assailant until he knocked her unconscious. Mina cringed at the sound of fist hitting jaw.

Mina suddenly smelled a whiff of wet dog, and found it disorienting to be coming from the back of a fully dressed man. *Think, Mina, think. How does this story end?*

Footsteps, car doors opening, and Mina felt herself falling to land on the metal floor of a delivery van. Scrambling to gain footing, she tried kicking at the man crawling in next to her in the van. Mina opened her mouth to scream, and an old rag quickly filled her mouth, followed by rope around her wrists. She pushed herself into a sitting position in the far corner of the truck.

"Just in case you get any ideas," Lonetree hissed into her ear. The van dipped as more people clambered in. Mina saw them lower Nan's unconscious body next to her. The engine turned over, and they were moving. Out the back window she could see the brick gym slowly getting smaller as they pulled away. What now?

As the van chugged along, Mina heard the distant hum of a far-off motor and barely gave it any thought until it grew louder the closer it came. She almost cried with relief when she saw a familiar black motorcycle pull up behind the delivery van and spotted Jared's shock of dark hair. The bike disappeared around the side of the van, and Mina mentally cheered for her hero. Jared would save them. She listened for the sounds of a struggle, but she was slammed into the side of the van as it swerved quickly to one side. Either they were trying to cut Jared off, or run him over. The van hit its brakes, and this time she was thrown against the driver's seat. She struggled to her knees and could see Jared out the front windshield. The driver picked up speed once more, to position the van next to Jared.

She screamed his name and could have sworn he looked her way into the darkened van, even though he couldn't possibly see her. The driver swerved, and she watched as the front headlight struck Jared's leg and he began to lose control of the motorcycle. Her heart was in her throat as she jumped forward between the seats and tried to pull the gearshift into Neutral with her tied hands.

The driver yelled angrily, and Mina felt herself picked up and tossed into the back of the van as it careened wildly. Quickly, it was under control and speeding along again.

"What did I tell you about interfering?" Grey Tail growled. "Just for that, I'm gonna kill him. Jared appeared behind the van once more, and Mina saw Grey Tail pick up a spare car battery from the truck bed and fling open the doors. The *whoosh* of air caught her hair as she struggled to see Jared behind him, to let him know that she was okay. As the truck swerved again, Grey Tail threw the car battery out at Jared but just missed him, growling in anger.

Next, Mina saw Jared do something crazy, pointing at Grey Tail and beckoning in challenge. Grey Tail leaned outside the van, fingers digging into the van door, leaving inch-wide holes in the frame. A howl split the night as he arched his back, preparing to lunge onto Jared's bike.

Suddenly the van slammed on its brakes, and Jared quickly veered left and then backward, giving the wolf a chance to lunge into his back. Mina watched in terror as two hundred pounds of muscle hit Jared from behind and knocked him from his bike. The men rolled several times across the pavement, and the last thing she saw amid the chaos was the wolf's claws ripping into Jared as they began to speed away.

CHAPTER 23

Mina screamed into the gag, and tears flowed freely from her eyes. Jared had risked his life for her, and now there would be no one to save her.

Dread. Hopelessness. Loss. All of it consumed her. Numbness took hold, and she didn't fight or struggle when a different wolf reached down to haul her over his shoulder. She barely registered that they were back at Babushka's Bakery.

Mina wasn't sure if she was surprised or not to see none other than B.J., Claire's great-grandson, climbing out from behind the wheel. Claire marched forward, holding open a side door marked "Deliveries Only" for them to pass through. It was cold and dark, and smelled of flour and diesel fumes. They removed Mina's gag but not her bindings.

"I'll start with the blonde one," Claire croaked out. She went over to Nan, hauled her up by her hair, and peered carefully into her unconscious face. Reaching out with a sun-marked, wrinkled hand, Claire rested it over Nan's mouth. Faint glowing lines began to pour out of Nan and into Claire through her hand.

Nan opened her eyes in fear as the process began, and she began to age in front of Mina. Her blue eyes turned gray, her ivory skin turned clear. Mina screamed as Nan went from sixteen to eighty-six in seconds. All the while, Claire seemed to reverse in age. Her hair grew out and became blonde. Her face filled out and she grew younger, but stopped when she reached about fifty.

Suddenly, Claire let Nan fall to the floor. "That's all I can take without killing her," Claire said, her voice stronger and louder than before. She turned to Mina with a predatory smile. "I know you don't want me to destroy her, so I suggest you give me the Grimoire now, before I finish with you."

Mina shrank back in fear.

"What did you expect? It's easier to take a few years off unsuspecting teenagers than to leave a dried-out corpse. To make this permanent, I need your life energy and the Grimoire. Give it to me now, or I will take what little years she has left. At least one of you will survive this."

Perhaps Claire thought she was scaring Mina into compliance, but she was really giving her the extra courage she needed. Claire moved toward Nan's feeble body and reached out a hand threateningly.

"No, wait!" Mina struggled to stand. "I'll give you the Grimoire, but I need to be somewhere more private."

"Don't take me for a fool, girl!" Claire grunted.

"I don't. It's just that…" Mina tried to play the part of a shy, reserved girl, which wasn't that hard for her. Blood rushed to her cheeks in embarrassment. "I strapped it in with my corset. I need to undress to get it."

Claire snorted and laughed at Mina's awkwardness. She pointed to a shelf piled high with cans of lard. "Behind there, but that is all the privacy I'll allow. Just so you know, there is nowhere to run, and nowhere to hide." She motioned, and Lonetree cut off Mina's bindings.

Mina bobbed her head and slowly walked behind the shelf, as if resigned to her doomed state. Once out of sight, she reached into her bodice and pulled out the Grimoire easily.

Opening it up, she was surprised to see the pages blank still, except for the first story she'd solved. She was hoping for a little bit of information.

"C'mon, I need your help!" she whispered to the book. "You're supposed to help me, and now would be an ideal time." The book was lifeless; there was no glow or hum. "Please! I beg you." Nothing.

Mina curled up on the floor and held the notebook to her chest. Images flooded in her mind, variations of children's books she'd read in the library. Their images panned through Mina's mind like a documentary on wolves, little girls, and then hunters.

She was waiting for a hunter to come save her, but that wasn't how it always worked. Sometimes Red saved her grandma from the wolves. The story had changed. They were in Grandma's house. "Babushka" was Russian for "Grandma," right? Mina hoped so. So Claire would have to be the grandma. No, that wasn't right. Claire was obviously the villain here. She peeked back over the corner to see Claire next to an old lady who was quaking in fear. Nan! Nan was now old enough to be Mina's grandma. The Story had worked that it out so she was little Red, who had to outsmart the wolves in Grandma's house to save her. Jared had said Claire's story was over. It was completed, just not finished yet. So Mina needed to focus on the villain in this story, which was not Claire but the wolves.

Mina had been waiting for Jared or Brody to save her, thinking that was what the story called for. But not if Mina had any say.

"I'm the hunter," Mina whispered to herself. "I'm now the hunter, not the hunted," she whispered louder. "I will not lose!" Mina grabbed tightly onto the notebook and began running toward the side wall and the closest Fae wolf. The wolf bared his teeth, but the book thrummed once, twice, and three times like a beating heart coming back to life.

Mina believed in the power of the tale. She knew that the Story needed Mina to grow in power. And just because she didn't understand how to use the Grimoire exactly didn't mean that it wouldn't help her if she believed. She had to trust herself.

Mina closed her eyes and pictured herself as a hunter, and just before she swung the book, the weapon she needed appeared in her hands. She opened her eyes in awe. The notebook had transformed into an ethereal battle axe of light. Mina giggled in a moment of pure insanity as she realized she must look like a crazy character from some anime film. The wolf howled when the light touched his skin. She saw the light burn through the human illusion to the wolf underneath.

Mina pulled the axe back once more, and swung again at the wolf. With each swipe, the creature howled and tried to dodge the glowing light from the axe.

He clawed at Mina, but she jumped away. With another swipe of the axe, another layer peeled from the Fae wolf, and he dissolved into thin air. Turning, Mina headed toward another wolf, but he panicked and ran down the hall, not wishing to be a part of the same fate.

Turning toward Claire, Mina held the axe and stepped forward threateningly. "Change her back!"

Claire's eyes squinted as she studied Mina. "I can't. And where in the world did you get that?"

"Change her back, or I'll use it. This is no ordinary axe."

"The Grimoire," Claire whispered, her eyes sparkling. She shrugged. "The only way I can help your friend is if you give me the book. Perhaps then we can find a way to extend her life. After all, she doesn't have Fae blood like me."

"No, I don't bel..." Mina couldn't finish, as she was knocked forward to the ground, the Grimoire flying out of her hands and sliding across the floor. It slowly changed back from an axe to a passive notebook lying at Claire's feet.

"Why, thank you." Claire reached down to pick it up. "I do so love it when things go my way. Don't you agree, Lonetree?"

Mina felt herself get pulled upward off the ground as Lonetree hauled her to the cold cement floor in front of Claire, grunting his assent.

Claire opened the notebook and frowned when she saw the unfinished sketch. "Come now." She shook it. "Show me my story. I saw the Fae copy when I was a child. I know this one records a duplicate. I want to see mine to make sure it gets the story right." Claire chuckled and flipped a few more pages, finally ripping out a page in anger. "Show me! Or I'll rip out more!" Unsatisfied, Claire finally tucked the Grimoire into her purse. "Never mind, there are other ways to make it talk. As long as you understand that this story doesn't have a happily ever after for Gretel."

Mina spoke up defiantly. "You're wrong!"

Claire glared at Mina. "What do you know?"

"I know your story. It's finished. You're destined to die. Whether it be today or tomorrow, it's already over. Nothing you do will change the final outcome."

"You stupid girl! Everything can be changed. Look how many times this story has progressed over the years."

"But we are no longer in your story. You're in mine. And in my tale, I win." Mina held up her chin in defiance. A small trickle of blood dripped down it onto her dress, a wound from getting tackled by Lonetree."

"I don't understand."

Banging doors and a few crashes later, Mina heard someone calling her name. It sounded like Brody. He must have seen Jared pull out of the school parking lot and followed. She needed to finish this tale, and finish it now.

"Do you want to know why your tale isn't in my copy of the book? It's because I finished your tale weeks ago. But the Story needed you for one more task. I don't have a living grandmother. So the Story kept you around long enough to create a grandmother for my current quest. It used you to satisfy the needs of a different tale, to create someone that I loved enough to risk my life for. Nothing more. And I finished that tale moments ago."

Mina stood up and walked over to Nan, who was lying on the cold floor. She held Nan close, hugging her. "I just killed the wolf and saved my dear grandmother. This tale is over. I won. Check and see." Mina pointed to the Grimoire as it began to glow. Slowly etched pencil sketches began to fill in a page that mirrored the surrounding scene. Mina knew that somewhere on the Fae plane, a similar picture was appearing in the Fae Book. She could almost hear an audible sigh coming from beyond. Claire dropped the notebook, and Mina saw the words "The End" appearing underneath the picture. With it came a loud rushing wind that rattled the windows, and she felt herself being pulled forward toward the Grimoire.

Mina gripped tightly onto Nan as the earth shook and shelves clanged. The room seemed to spin, and bright light burst from Nan's body. Mina screamed in fear, worried she was losing her best friend. She, too, was being pulled toward the Grimoire, and Mina wasn't sure she could hold on.

Suddenly strong hands grabbed her, and Mina recognized Brody as he embraced her and pushed her to the floor, covering her with his body. He must have noticed her disappearance and seen Jared take off running. Like Jared, he must have followed the van here.

"I've got you! I won't let you go. I promise!"

Mina's eyes stung as she watched the book float off the ground and begin to absorb a scared Lonetree and a screaming Claire. Mina's teeth chattered in fright as Claire reached toward Mina. Whether she wanted Mina's help or the last few years of her life, Mina didn't know. But Claire was sucked into the pages of the Grimoire.

The book fell open the floor with a loud *plop*. When the wind, the noise, and the ground quit moving, Mina tried to push herself off Nan but was held captive by Brody's body.

Brody moved off Mina and looked her over for injuries. Other than a cut on her face and a few bruises, she looked okay. "You're all right! Thank God!" He pulled her into an embrace and kissed her. The kiss tasted salty and sweet. "I'm never letting you out of my sight again," he whispered, kissing her head. Mina pulled away to check on Nan.

Nan's skin was still glowing, and she was slowly turning back to her normal self. Mina felt her skin start to prickle, the same buildup of power she felt whenever the Story interacted on their plane. She looked around in apprehension and couldn't find a source. Then she felt it coming from the Grimoire. Mina walked over to the book and could feel a buildup of power before it snapped closed with finality, knocking her and Brody off their feet with its power.

Mina looked over at Brody, who was now lying prostrate on the floor next to Nan; he looked to be out cold.

"Brody!" Mina screamed, running to him. Mina ran her fingers over his tanned skin and around his head, looking for large bumps or bruises. He seemed to be fine.

"Gosh! Stop pawing over him already and help me up," Nan mumbled sleepily as she tried to pull herself up. She looked around the room. "What are we doing here?"

"Don't you remember?" Mina asked. "Claire from Babushka's showed up at the dance and brought us here."

"Babushka's what? I have no idea what you're talking about. And wait – are we missing out on the dance?! And what is *he* doing here?"

Mina was dumbfounded. Nan didn't remember anything. Was this a joke or a side effect of being healed too quickly? "Don't you remember? He was my date."

"Um, yeah right. I distinctly remember we both had decided to go stag. He was Savannah's date, not yours." Nan stood up and began to limp around the room.

"But I saved his life at this bakery, three weeks ago. There was a big rally and we started dating, and he even gave me a cell phone, see." Mina looked around on the floor for her phone, but couldn't remember where she had lost it.

"You? Owning a cell phone? Ha! That will be the day. Are you sure you're feeling okay? I don't know how to tell you this, but there's no way we went on a field trip here. Look at this place—it hasn't been open in years."

Nan was right. Mina looked around, and what once was a working factory with whitewashed walls and stainless-steel equipment was now a dank, dirty, broken-down warehouse. Broken crates and spray paint littered the inside, and Mina could have sworn she saw a rat.

It was like the Bakery had never existed. The Story had created it all, set it all up. Once the tale was completed, it had erased everything, leaving no lasting impact on the human world. Mina started to feel her chest heave with pain. Her hand went to her heart as she turned to look at Brody. It wasn't real, none of it. Had the Story created his feelings for her? Maybe it hadn't, but would he remember?

Nan was still talking. "If something that cool had happened, don't you think I would be the first to know about it? I would have, like, a million followers on Twitter!" She had moved over to the red notebook and nudged it with her foot before picking it up.

"Don't touch that!" Mina cried. Rushing over, she snatched it from her best friend's hands. Nan backed away, hurt by Mina's harsh tone. "Sorry. But don't you think we should get out of here before we get in trouble?"

"And we had better get Brody. I don't want to be the one to explain to Savannah White that we took off with her date."

Nan was right. Brody began to stir.

Mina took two steps back from Brody as he leaned forward and looked around at his surroundings. He looked dazed, especially when he saw the two girls he was with. Mina held her breath as his gaze finally came to rest on her. She was waiting for a spark, a glimmer of recognition, and for his eyes to crinkle up in happiness when he saw her. There was nothing. He looked at her like a stranger before resting his cool blue eyes on Nan.

"Um, I know you, right?" He stood up and dusted off his pants.

"Yep," Nan answered crisply.

"Nan Taylor?" he asked.

"Right again…ding, ding, ding. Give the boy a prize," Nan snorted out as she continued looking for clues as to why they were here.

"What are we doing here?" Brody asked. He sounded helplessly lost.

"I think we've been punked. And this had better not be one of your ideas, Brody. Now, if you don't mind, I would like to get back to the dance." She walked over to Mina and looped her hand through Mina's arms. "Let's get out of here, prom date. This place gives me the creeps."

Mina nodded and followed in step with Nan, grateful for her best friend's support. She was doing everything she could to hold back her tears, but she couldn't even see where she was walking. She let Nan lead her out the back and toward a waiting limo, the means by which Brody had mysteriously appeared. Without caring whose car it was, she marched forward, opened up the door, and climbed inside. Brody walked behind them slowly and slid in after closing the limo door. He knocked on the window for the driver to pull away.

Mina scooted as far away from him as she could, hoping the darkness would hide her tears. She wiped her chin and came away with blood. Sighing, she tried wiping it on her dirty and stained dress, which was ruined anyway. She didn't remember that from the fairy tale.

Mina looked up when she felt someone staring, and caught Brody's gaze before he quickly looked away, as if embarrassed. Mina tried to stare out the window and compose herself. But fresh new tears began to fall as she realized Jared was gone forever, too.

Brody cleared his throat. "Uh, I'm sorry. Here." He slid down the bench and handed her a handkerchief out of his pocket. She almost laughed at the gesture. Who uses handkerchiefs anymore?

Mina shook her head, scared to look at him for fear of crying harder.

"Your name's Mina, right?"

Mina bobbed her head.

"Well, Mina, you've got a cut on your chin, and I think it needs to be looked at." He leaned forward and gently pressed the cloth to Mina's wound. "I'm sorry. I don't know what happened tonight, but obviously it was some sort of prank. Rest assured I will find out how we ended up here. And I'm sorry you got hurt."

He was talking to her as if he barely knew her. Were all of those kisses and feelings they had for each other gone? They couldn't be, could they? Mina was too scared to ask, too scared to get turned down and made into a fool. But she was used to being the fool, right? Just when Mina opened her mouth to tell Brody the truth, Nan shouted from the seat down by the minibar.

"Look, sparkling cider! And it's open."

CHAPTER 24

"Ugh, the water polo team!" Nan fumed on Monday during lunch. "I hate those guys." It had turned out that the Story seemed to like Nan's suggestion that they'd been pranked, and had used it to explain their appearance at the factory. Supposedly, the polo team, on a dare, had kidnapped Brody and two random girls to rile up Savannah, who was furious when her boyfriend was stolen during the dance. It was meant to look like a seamy affair, and got a big laugh for most of the students, except for Mina. She was mortified.

Nan couldn't stay mad long, as her tweets about the encounter nearly doubled her followers on Twitter. "I must admit, seeing Savannah's face as we stepped out of the limo was priceless. I gained major points among the Savannah haters." Nan smiled and waved cattily at Savannah, who was nuzzling with Brody three tables away. Savannah fumed at Nan, who just laughed.

Mina hung her head and refused to look. She had been getting odd looks from Brody, but they weren't reassuring. If anything, they made her more nervous. He looked uncomfortable, like he was forgetting something but couldn't put his finger on it. And probably never would.

Mina had returned home that night to find her family asleep in bed. She changed out of her dress and threw it in the closet, at least glad that her clothes now encompassed more of the color spectrum besides red. She went to her dresser and pulled out her notebook of Unaccomplishments and Epic

Disasters, searching for her previous entry about Brody. It was still there, so she knew it hadn't been a dream. The Story had at least left her that.

Now her mother's conversation regarding Brody forgetting all about her made sense. Her mother had known this would happen, but instead of telling her that their relationship would end, she had given Mina a few days of happiness. She wished now that her mother had told her. It would have saved her some of the heartache, though not all of it.

She'd sneaked out the fire escape and waited on her rooftop retreat all night, praying that Jared would magically appear to annoy her. He would be so proud that she had completed three tales. He never showed. Mina even looked over the Grimoire. There were no words, just pictures that depicted the three completed tales. But they were faded, barely discernible, as if Mina had used up the book's power in the battle against Claire and the Fae wolves. All of the power that used to hum in the Grimoire had disappeared. Scared, Mina carried the book everywhere with her. She even started sleeping with it under her pillow. Even now it was inside her hoodie, close to her body.

Mina looked over at Nan, who had pulled out a compact and was staring at her forehead with a frown. She hadn't spoken in at least five minutes, acting completely out of character for Mina's happy-go-lucky, carefree friend. "What's wrong?" Mina asked.

Nan made a face into her mirror. "Oh, nothing. It's just that I can't get over the feeling that I have more wrinkles than normal. Look at me—does this look like an age spot to you?" Nan opened her eyes wide and leaned forward comically toward Mina.

"No." Mina laughed.

"How about wrinkles?" Nan scrunched up her face and created too many wrinkles to count.

"Well, now that you mention it, I think you should enroll for the senior citizen discount. I'm sure you could pass," Mina replied.

"I knew it!" Nan gasped, pushing her favorite cupcake away and pulling out some age-defying lotion from her purse. She began to lather her skin with urgency.

Mina started laughing, but gasped out loud when an intense heat flared up in her midsection from the Grimoire. She put her fingers to her belly, and felt the Grimoire begin to pulse with life. The hair on the back of Mina's neck began to move, and her body began to tingle. She frantically looked around the room in preparation for an attack. She even stood up and put her back to the wall, ready to defend Nan.

Nan's phone beeped. She pulled it out and let out a slow whistle of appreciation. "Well, look at that! Seems we have a new student, and he's a hot one. Want to see his picture?" Nan held the phone so Mina could look, but she didn't. She could feel power building behind her.

Mina turned in dread and then froze, her heart beating loudly in her ears. He was right there, standing mere feet from her.

Jared.

Turn the page for a preview sample of

The first book in Chanda Hahn's
NEW fantasy series!

~I~

When I first awoke in the darkness that was my prison cell, I was brave, fearless and I still had enough fight in me to question the rules. But after my third beating by Scar Lip, I learned to hold my tongue while in his presence. After my first taste of torture on the machine, I learned obedience. Down in this hell, silence was more than golden; it was the difference between life and death. And where we were, there was a whole lot of death.

The sound of a distant door slamming snapped my mind back to the present. Footsteps slowed and our cell door opened with an ominous creak. The light from the hall fell across my bruised face making my eyes flinch in pain. A small whimper and the rustle of straw drew my attention to the other forgotten occupant of my cell, a small girl named Cammie. She pathetically tried to scoot away and put as much distance between her and the man about to enter our cell.

My mouth formed the word, NO, as an ugly bulldog of a man ducked under the too short door frame. I knew without looking it was Scar Lip. He had a crooked nose, dark unwashed hair and cruel black eyes that hid beneath a furrowed brow. He smiled in delight at Cammie's attempt to evade him, which made the scar that transected his top lip stand out in paleness.

The smell that accompanied him was a mixture of sweat and rot, which permeated from the layers of dried and crusted blood that coated his blacksmith's apron. He had come to take one of us to Raven.

Drips of sweat beaded across my forehead as the footsteps drew closer. It was too soon, I wasn't strong enough for another session on the machine. I groaned when I saw the smear of blood coating the back of my hand, leftover from last night's experiment. I knew that if he chose me again, I wouldn't survive. I tried to raise my head from the cold stone floor as he came closer to stand over my prone form. But a sudden wave of fear made me vomit what little was left in my stomach.

Scar Lip paused over my dry heaving body and backed away in disgust. When the convulsions stopped, I heard him move towards Cammie, and the sounds of scuffling as she crawled farther into the darkness of the cell hoping its shadows would hide her from his gaze. It was no use; all she did was back herself into a corner.

Cammie whimpered, "Please!...don't," and was smacked in the face by Scar Lip.

"No talking! You know the rules," he sneered.

Her lipped quivered and a small amount of blood appeared at the side of her mouth. She tried to wipe at it with the back of her hand, but only smeared it across her chin. She bit her bottom lip between her teeth to keep any more sound from coming forth.

"That's better," he growled. "The Raven has a new experiment to try and needs another volunteer." Scar Lip grabbed Cammie by the arms and dragged her out into the hall; her feet twisting and fighting behind her, trying to slow his efforts. She hadn't lost her fight, but if she survived the week in this pit, she would.

I raised my hand towards them as if by that one action alone I could protect her and stop what was about to happen. The large cell door shut with a thud, and I waited to hear if the lock turned. It did. I counted the steps as Scar lip dragged Cammie up the stairs through another door; mentally tracing the intricate path they would take until they came to a huge iron door that once opened, would let out a smell of iron, sulfur and death. I knew from experience that a table waited behind that door with cold iron shackles and as well as... I shivered at the mental picture that formed of the nameless machine they used to experiment on us.

When the sound of the door at the top of the stairs closed, the pain in my chest exploded because I was holding my breath. I cried in relief that I wasn't going to be tortured and experimented on again, that I survived one more day. I dropped my head to the floor and let the grief pour out of my body in loud aching sobs, as I realized in shame that I was happy he chose Cammie.

Read the rest of Thalia's story in **The Iron Butterfly***!*

***

Chanda Hahn takes her experience as a children's pastor, children's librarian and bookseller to write compelling and popular fiction for teens. She was one of Amazon's top customer favorite authors of 2012 and is an ebook bestseller in five countries.

She was born in Seattle, Washington, grew up in Nebraska, and currently resides in Portland, Oregon with her husband and their twin children; Aiden and Ashley.

Visit Chanda Hahn's website to learn more about her other forthcoming books. **www.chandahahn.com**

Also by Chanda Hahn

Unfortunate Fairy Tale Series
UnEnchanted
Fairest
Fable

The Iron Butterfly Series
The Iron Butterfly
The Steele Wolf
The Silver Siren

Acknowledgements

I want to say a special thanks to everyone who took part in the process of helping me with the UnEnchanted, whether you were a reader, editor, encourager, or critic. Thanks to Philip Hahn, Steve Hahn, Alison Brace & Christy Wynkoop. Also to my parents, Mike and Chris DiPaolo, who kept telling me to publish and publish soon. I have the best team ever.

CPSIA information can be obtained at www.ICGtesting.com
Printed in the USA
LVOW12s2131200913

353472LV00001B/252/P